PROMISED LAND

A Novel

Karel Schoeman

translated by
Marion V. Friedmann

SUMMIT BOOKS
NEW YORK

Copyright © 1972 by Karel Schoeman
Translation Copyright © 1978 by Marion V. Friedmann
All rights reserved
including the right of reproduction
in whole or in part in any form
Published by *Summit Books*
A Simon & Schuster Division of Gulf & Western Corporation
Simon & Schuster Building
Rockefeller Center
1230 Avenue of the Americas
New York, New York 10020
Manufactured in the United States of America
Printed and bound by The Maple Press Company

1 2 3 4 5 6 7 8 9 10

Library of Congress Cataloging in Publication Data

Schoeman, Karel.
Promised land.

Translation of Na die geliefde land.

I. Title.
PZ4.S3625Pr   [PT6592.29.C5]   839.3′6′35   78-6788

ISBN 0-671-40031-2

'Who are you?' the man called out.

Blinded by the sudden light, George shielded his eyes with his hand. 'I'm looking for the road to Rietvlei,' he answered.

There was no immediate response. Then, from where he was standing at the top of the steps leading to the house, the man moved forward a pace and the light of the torch he was gripping danced across the empty farmyard. 'Who are you?' he asked again. 'Where do you come from?'

How was he, then and there, to explain in the middle of the yard, with the light in his eyes, the interrogator himself invisible behind it?

'I've come from abroad,' he said.

The man with the torch was silent, as if he were hesitating in the doorway trying to make something of the information.

'I'm on my way to Rietvlei,' George went on. 'It grew dark sooner than I expected, and I seem to have missed a turn-off somewhere.' Still the man remained silent, waiting, the light unsteady in his hand.

'The farm belonged to my mother,' George said. 'She died recently and I've come to put her affairs in order.'

'Are you Anna Neethling's son?'

'Yes,' he said and, when his answer had been considered and digested, the man switched off the torch. 'I didn't know,' he said. 'I didn't know that Anna was dead. We heard that she had gone overseas, she and her husband, but so many people have gone abroad and one never hears anything about them again.'

'Is it far to Rietvlei?' George asked.

'There's no-one there, you can't go there.'

'Surely there's a caretaker?'

'There's no-one at Rietvlei, the farm has been abandoned for years. You can't go there now.' He opened the door behind him and a weak light from the house shone out obliquely, so that it was possible to see him, a well-built man in his late fifties, dressed in khaki working-clothes.

'Hattingh,' he introduced himself, and shook hands with a powerful grip. 'When did you arrive?'

'Yesterday. I got to the town this afternoon and hired a car: I couldn't find anyone willing to drive me out here and I couldn't 'phone the farm. There seems to be no telephone.'

'No-one has lived at Rietvlei for years,' the old man repeated while he stared searchingly at George. 'Were you born overseas?'

'No, here.'

'You speak Afrikaans like a foreigner.'

'I was only a child when we left here: I grew up abroad.' This was an investigation, he realized, to see if he really was what he claimed to be and to ascertain if he could be trusted, and he wondered what password or proof of identity would satisfy the suspicious old farmer before him.

'When I was a child,' he said, 'we used to visit my grandparents on the farm, but I hardly remember it now: I don't even know how to get there. They gave me directions in the town but I seem to have lost my way.'

'There were always children at the farm, all the grandchildren, and lots of nieces, nephews, cousins, with children of their own. Lottie loved to have children about her.'

'I can just remember her,' said George and sought in the shards and debris of his memory, among dreamlike images and the rhythm of sentences of which the words were long lost. 'There was a dam, and fig-trees.'

'Goodness knows where all those children are today — people disappear without leaving a trace. It's almost as though they never existed.'

'My parents also lost nearly all contact with the family. My mother did hear that her parents had died, but only months afterwards.'

Hattingh stood there as if weighing something over. 'Come in,' he said then, a password recognized somewhere among the other words, and George followed him up the steps to the house.

'This is Anna Neethling's son,' Hattingh said. 'She was the daughter of Uncle George and Aunt Lottie — you people probably don't remember her any more. He's come from overseas to look at the farm: his mother is dead.'

Only now, as he remained standing on the threshold of the room, did George realize that there were other people in the house. In the dim electric light he saw three young men immediately in front of him, all dressed like Hattingh, standing shoulder to shoulder as if offering resistance to his entry. When Hattingh had spoken they moved apart and he could see the room, and in it a large table, a stove, and a woman who came forward out of the half-shadow while the others greeted him. She wiped her hand hastily on her apron and it felt soft and delicate in his after the firm handshake of the men. 'We'll eat now,' said Hattingh, and she turned away, busying herself with pots and plates. These must be Hattingh's wife and sons, thought George, although the relationship had not been explained. Someone else, in working-clothes like the others, came in while Hattingh was indicating where he should sit. It was only when George took the outstretched hand that he could make out, in the poor light, by features and movements that the newcomer was a girl.

Around the table, where they had all come to sit, an uncomfortable silence prevailed after Hattingh, with bent head, had muttered a prayer: there was only the sound of spoons against the plates as the meal was served.

'We live simply here,' said Hattingh. 'You'll no doubt be used to other things abroad.' He was stating a fact, not offering an excuse.

'Everything in Africa is strange to me,' said George. 'But I want to see it as it is.'

There was dry porridge and a dish of stewed beans; the girl got up and brought a jug of water to the table, cold, clear spring-water. The table was covered with a patterned oil-cloth at which he stared in the silence. The plates didn't match and most of them were chipped or cracked, but special plates with gold rims had been given to him as guest, relics of an old, lost dinner-service.

He heard only the clatter of cutlery, and looked up. The young men opposite him lowered their eyes and stared at their plates as they went on eating. He saw a cupboard against the wall, a shelf, pictures of national leaders and politicians whom he recognized from history-books; he was suddenly overwhelmed by exhaustion after his long journey and by an aversion from these silent people in their worn clothes, the food, the ill-lit room and the strangeness and unexpectedly poverty-stricken appearance of everything.

The woman moved restlessly to and from the table, never sitting for long, busy fetching and carrying, serving the menfolk. He saw her eyes fixed on him, solicitously, questioningly, faded eyes in a weary face, as if she had aged too early, years before her time. Then she smiled to herself as she continued to look at him.

'One can see whose grandson you are,' she said with satisfaction. 'One can see you're Anna's son. I met her only a few times and a long time ago at that, but I remember her well. People. always said she was the prettiest girl in the district.'

This was the first time she had spoken to him. The young men did not look up, but in some way her words seemed to release the tension behind their silence. So, he thought, did their acceptance of him lie in this: his inherited features, the mouth and eyes of a young woman who had grown old in loneliness and was now dead?

'It was when I was still engaged and visited this farm. She was at Rietvlei with Aunt Lottie: she was already married then. I still remember how beautifully she

dressed: all the women were talking about her.'
Recollections of the past had make her talkative.

'She rode well,' said Hattingh. 'I can still see her
galloping through the veld on one of Uncle George's
horses.'

His mother — on horseback over the veld, her hair
tossed by the wind. And a room, in which magazines lay
on the floor and the ash-trays were always full; her
coughing, her fine features gradually marked with pain;
the ever heavier make-up with which she tried to hide
the inexorable progress of time; bottles and syringes on a
little table next to her bed. Outside were the great
mountains, rounding off, completing the doll's-house
landscape. '... Those damned mountains!' she would
call out and push aside the travelling-rug with which he
was trying to cover her legs. There were paintings on the
walls, landscapes they had brought with them when they
left, pictures at which he looked without recognition. In
those last months she too no longer looked at them.

The woman was still staring at him across the table.
'You're tired,' she said with concern.

'I didn't sleep well. I couldn't sleep in the 'plane, and
last night in the hotel everything was still so strange I
couldn't settle down.'

She looked questioningly at her husband. 'You can
stay and sleep here,' he said.

'Won't it be inconvenient for you?'

'I just have to make the bed,' Mrs Hattingh said and
stood up.

'We live simply, as I've told you,' said Hattingh, 'but
that's because circumstances are difficult. We haven't
forgotten how to be hospitable.'

The girl had fetched the coffee and now came round

the table pouring it out for them; the young men pushed back their chairs and spoke from time to time among themselves without looking at George again.

'You can't go back to town now,' said Hattingh. 'It's not safe to drive around alone in the dark, and in any case there isn't even a decent hotel. We've still got some talking to do: you must tell us about your mother, your parents.'

The woman returned and went and stood behind her husband's chair, her hand on its back. 'We go to bed early,' he said, 'because we've got to get up early: there's enough work on the farm, more than enough. I'll show you where your room is. Tomorrow we'll talk again.'

Stiff from cold and the long journey, unsteady on his feet with weariness, George nodded at the young people around the table, who looked up but made no gesture, and followed Hattingh along the dark passage to his room.

Approaching the farm he had seen in the headlights only the road before him, and then a gate, trees and the blank wall of the farmhouse where he had stopped to ask the way. Now he could see the deserted yard, the outbuildings and sheds with rusted corrugated-iron roofs, a tractor and petrol-drums. It was already late morning but in the house all was quiet and there was no-one outside. He walked aimlessly around the yard and past the outbuildings to a barbed-wire fence where he stopped to look at the land beyond the last sparse blue-gum trees: the prospect was bare, empty, desolate, the low line of the veld uninterrupted by hill or house. He stared at it, not quite taking in what he saw, and waited for some revelation, some explanation of his mother's love of this land, her longing, her fidelity to which he had been a witness all his life without himself ever being touched by it. But no revelation came: he found only solitude and silence, self-sufficient facts, as it were, before him.

The girl whom he had seen in the kitchen the previous night crossed the yard with a loaded sack on her shoulders. She stopped momentarily as if he had frightened her, but then she recognized him.

'Can I carry that for you?' he asked, but she shook her head.

'I'm only going to the store-room,' she said and walked on.

The hired car stood where he had left it the previous night and he walked to it, the only familiar thing here. Where was everybody, he wondered, and how was he to take leave of them? It was time, after all, to continue his journey. But the girl had disappeared and not come back; the kitchen door stood ajar, the threshold deserted.

In a silence in which there was hardly the call of a bird, every sound must have been audible, yet Hattingh was suddenly there, almost near enough to touch him, before George looked up and saw him.

'Are you having a look around? The farm's been badly neglected in the last few years: it's no longer what it was when I began farming, but we must be grateful that we still have it, neglected or not. It's family land, an inheritance from my great-grandfather, but in his day they still had the money and labour to maintain it. He wouldn't think much of us if he were to see it today; even my late father wouldn't be pleased with it. He died at a time when everything was still going well.' He stood silently, reflecting, his hands in his pockets, and then he asked George to come in and eat.

Where the woman had been, George didn't know, but when they came in they found her busy in the kitchen, where there was a place laid for him at one end of the table. While he ate, she remained standing near him to pour his coffee, pass him things and see that he had what he needed.

'I'm sure you're used to better food overseas,' she

said.

'My wife keeps on making excuses for everything,' Hattingh said. 'I don't do it any more. You come from abroad but you know how things are here; you'll take us as you find us.'

'We never heard much about what happened here. We seldom saw anybody who could tell us what was going on.'

'Were your parents homesick?' asked Mrs Hattingh.

'My mother was, at any rate towards the end as she got older and became an invalid.'

'When did she die?' Mrs Hattingh asked, not looking at him.

'A few months ago.'

'And your father, is he still alive?'

'He died quite a few years ago.'

'He was in the diplomatic corps, wasn't he?'

'Yes. He was sent overseas when I was still a child, so I grew up abroad.'

'You people were lucky to get away in time,' said Hattingh. 'But prominent people and the rich left early, on the whole, almost before we ordinary folk realized that there was anything wrong. With their trunks and crates, and their money in foreign banks.'

'They were afraid,' said George.

'Yes, of course, and they probably had reason to be, but there were others who were afraid and remained nevertheless.' Slowly he began to fill his pipe while he spoke. 'There are two sorts of people in this country: those who stayed because they couldn't get away, and those who stayed even though they could.'

'Which is the larger group?' said George.

'What do you think? It's only a handful who decided

willingly to stick it out, but they're the cream of our people, those of them who are left.'

His wife waited impatiently for him to finish. 'Do you know many Afrikaners overseas?' she asked.

'My father worked among Afrikaners abroad in his last years; he helped them with money and work and documents and so forth. And my parents also entertained a lot: there were always visitors at the house.'

'Do you by any chance know the Hugo's?' Mrs Hattingh asked eagerly. 'Danie Hugo and his family, the Judge's son?'

'I think they're living in America; he's working as an engineer and I believe they've got on well.'

'Karin Hugo was one of my best friends. And Mona Oosthuizen, Mona and Nico?' She came to sit opposite him at the table asking about one person after another almost faster than he could answer: relations and connections, school-friends, fellow-students, acquaintances. Those she named had been people of substance in the old days or important in academic, legal and political circles, and most of them were known to him. He recalled introductions at parties and at dinners, whispered information given, the old yellowing labels which each person wore as identification, like the tags on plants and young shrubs in a garden. 'Senator Lindeman. . .', 'Professor Van den Heever. . :', 'She was a Miss du Plessis. . .' The titles usually meant nothing any more and the whole system of reference had collapsed long ago, but still they clung to their titles and the old, familiar framework, on the steep dark stairway of reality, as one might cling to a railing.

Mrs Hattingh sat with her hands folded on the table before her, dredging her memory for names, smiling

with wonderment at the fact that George knew them all
and hardly even trying to follow what he was telling her.
'He made a good marriage,' she said, interrupting him.
'Erna's father had about four or five farms. We were at
the wedding, do you remember, Father?' Without
giving her husband a chance to answer, she went on: 'It
was a slap-up affair, I don't know how many Ministers
came and Army people; there were something like seven
hundred guests, I think.'

She didn't really want to know what had become of
these people, George realized. For her too, the past —its
titles revoked, its impressive-sounding appointments
abolished— was more important than the alien and
incomprehensible present. In her drab face there was
suddenly colour and her eyes grew bright as the long-
withheld words poured out.

Hattingh sat and listened to what George had to say,
but he began to get restless during his wife's monologue.
Then he stood up. 'Well, I must go and work,' he said.
She hesitated, her narrative interrupted in midstream.

'I must go too,' said George. They looked at him,
obviously taken by surprise.

'Where to?' asked Hattingh.

'I must go on, to Rietvlei, make arrangements. . .'

'Why in such a hurry? I tell you there's nothing at
Reitvlei, it's been abandoned for years.'

'I very much want to see it again.'

'There's time enough for that. You can't want to go so
soon: we've hardly had time for a proper talk. There's so
much you still have to tell us.'

'And there are people in the district who'll want to see
you,' said Mrs Hattingh. 'People who knew Uncle
George and Aunt Lottie, who remember your mother. . .'

'I can't recall when we last had a visitor,' said Hattingh. 'People don't drive around any more in this part of the world; even the neighbours who stayed on don't visit often like they used to. You can surely stay here with us for a few days. How long have you come for?'

'I've taken only a week's leave,' said George. 'My return flight is already booked.'

'Are there things you want to do here, apart from visiting Rietvlei?'

'I've made no plans. I thought I might drive around a bit, see something of the country, perhaps even track down some of my parents' family.'

'What would anyone want to travel around for now?' said Hattingh. 'Nothing is like it was, and as for your family — it's better not to ask too many questions: you'll make difficulties for yourself and for others. You'd better stay with us.'

'Will you?' Mrs Hattingh spoke with a certain urgency.

'It's very kind of you. I could perhaps stay a little longer if it wouldn't put you out.'

'There's after all still such a thing as hospitality,' said Hattingh. 'There are still traditions which must be maintained.'

Breakfast was over and Mrs Hattingh began to clear the table. George followed Hattingh outside.

'In which direction is Rietvlei?' he asked.

Hattingh gestured. 'It's that way,' he said, 'about ten miles by road. You took the right turn-off last evening: you should just have continued on that road. But there's plenty of time to go there,' he added, as he started walking off towards his work. 'You can drive over there if you feel like it. Perhaps my wife could drive with you and visit Aunt Miemie at Moedersgift. It's just this side of Rietvlei.'

He called the last words over his shoulder. George remained standing next to the wall of the house while the wind blew across the yard and the blue-gum trees surged restlessly. It was a dull, overcast day. Where was the sun, he wondered, irritated as he had been yesterday by the poverty and drabness of everything he saw, the abandoned look of the house and yard, and the loose sheets of corrugated iron which began to clatter somewhere on the roof of one of the outbuildings. He had always remembered it as sunny, as it was on the calendar photographs: blue skies, bright clouds; peaches and water-melons in abundance; laughing natives in animal skins and beads; white beaches; lions in the long grass. The wind whirled dust into his eyes.

Why should he stay here, on this isolated farm with people he didn't know, who had welcomed him only because he relieved their loneliness? On the other hand, what sense was there in trying to see, in the few days at his disposal, the whole vast country? He would remain, he thought; he'd go to Rietvlei and then leave. After all, it was what he had come for.

Mrs Hattingh stood in front of the window, looking out. 'It's going to rain,' she said abstractedly. 'I wanted to wash the windows today, but I'd better wait. Sometimes one wonders if it's worth the trouble.'

'Can I do anything for you?' asked George.

'No, nothing at all. If you feel like it you can sit here and talk to me.' She shuffled back and forth in the kitchen in worn-out felt slippers, now opening a cupboard, now putting something away, now looking

for something. 'One's always busy with housework.'
She sighed. 'When I think that my mother-in-law used
to have five women working for her in the house, and
more when she wanted to spring-clean. At such times
Uncle Willem used to get out of the way and go and eat
at the neighbours'.'

'Have you lived here long?'

'We came when Johannes was still a baby. I don't
come from farming folk, myself. We lived in the city,
my husband worked there and earned a good living.' She
spread an old blanket over the table. 'But when the
troubles began we thought it safer to be on the farm: we
had two small children and the situation was so
uncertain. . .' She threw a sheet over the blanket and
slowly smoothed it. She just wants to talk, thought
George, just stand by herself and express all the
bottled-up griefs and grievances, scarcely aware of him
as she leaned over the table. There were no longer any
buttons on her cardigan, and her hair was pinned up
untidily. Only her face still bore traces of an earlier
delicacy and beauty.

'I'm not used to this sort of life,' she said sharply as if
defending herself against unspoken criticism. 'When I
was a girl I never had to do anything in the house, and
when I married we always kept servants. I never
expected that one day we'd live like this. It was forced
on me, I learned the hard way. When I left school, I
went to University. My father wanted me to study — he
didn't live to see what became of all my education. But it
was fun.' Her face lit up at the recollection. 'We were a
happy lot, we young students: the Marais's, and Ben
Meyer and Karin. Yes, all those we were talking about
this morning, and others: Leon Grobbelaar, who was

arrested later, and Len Botes who was killed during the troubles. I'm sure you've never heard of him but in his time he was a brilliant student. We always used to play tennis at his parents' —he was a good player— and he took me out a few times in our first year. There wasn't anything between us: we just went dancing or to the cinema. . .' Her mind elsewhere, she stroked the sheet over the table in front of her, the ironing she'd wanted to do —sheets, handkerchiefs, khaki shirts— forgotten. George hardly listened to the familiar tale. How often had he heard the same thing before, with minor changes of detail: the roll-call of names; the incidents enacted on tennis-courts or beside swimming-pools, in boardrooms or at meetings of the Senate; the enumeration of friends, achievements, possessions, conquests; the details of distinctions gained and profits made. Over the coffee-cups, the cocktail glasses, over liqueurs, in his parents' house or the houses of friends, the same recollections were called up, the same facts endlessly repeated, part of the investment on which exiles had to exist in unfamiliar surroundings. But those were people who had left and survived, separated by time, distance and indescribable experiences from this farm-woman in her faded jersey: the past was all they had in common, the memory of times past all that still bound them together.

Somewhere at the end of the passage a door slammed. Mrs Hattingh gave no sign of hearing it, but she broke off her narrative and the smile faded slowly from her face. Still lost in thought she continued to pluck at the sheet.

'I must bake today,' she said. 'I must bake a cake, seeing that we have a visitor.'

Please don't go to any trouble on my account.'

'It's no trouble; why should it be a trouble?' She held up a shirt. 'You must just look around in the house, do as you please. Perhaps you'll find something to read somewhere: there are still some old magazines. . .' She had suddenly withdrawn from him and went to the stove to fetch a flat-iron, his presence forgotten.

There was really no reason for him to have undertaken this trip: for one week it was hardly worth the effort, and problems in connection with the farm could have been dealt with by letter. If he were older and still remembered this country clearly, he would probably prefer memories to a confrontation with the new reality, and if he were younger and had no memories at all he would not have felt any bond or need to return. But he had just been old enough to be able to remember the place or at any rate to remember something which he thought of as "Africa", and which evoked in him mixed feelings of love, homesickness and curiosity. And so why shouldn't he have availed himself of the opportunity to come back, even for a few days, to try to recapture the dimly-remembered past, to try and find again the reality, and to resolve for himself all his conflicting feelings, among which were love and loyalty?

He had come for a week, not even for a week. Already it was his third day in the country; time was passing —swiftly, surely— while he walked along the passage of this unknown house, opening doors one by one. A few days more and he would have to return without having learned anything or come any closer to decoding a single one of innumerable secrets.

He had enough to do, he thought, and hesitated on a threshold, his hand on the doorknob; it was only with difficulty that he had managed to take the week off for

his sentimental, senseless journey. The house in which
his mother had died was still exactly as she had left it:
there were many things he had to sort, put in order,
arrange; he had postponed it long enough. Abstractedly
as he thought about these things, he surveyed the rooms
of the farmhouse without giving his full attention to
what he found in them, little. as it was — most of the
large rooms stood empty or were apparently used only
for storage. It was a large, high-ceilinged house, and the
scattered furniture looked lost in the spaciousness: a
single cupboard with a discoloured mirror, a bed, a table
and chairs in the middle of a room, a battered desk with
a roll-top lid. Some pieces of furniture were old and
dilapidated relics of vanished affluence and the newer, chea-
per furniture was not in keeping with them: the kitchen-
table with its formica top, chairs with aluminium
frames, imitation leather or wood and garish plastic.
Like the furniture the pictures were an uneasy mixture
of old and new: photographs from magazines, colour
prints of flowers and landscapes, jostling with older
photographs of leaders and national heroes among
heavily-framed portraits of solemn men and women in
their best clothes. These rooms must be the bedrooms of
the family, he realized, but he had to search for traces of
the inhabitants. Only single objects, glimpsed almost by
chance —a comb, a handkerchief, a pencil— indicated
the presence of people in this abandoned house.

There was still so much to do, he thought, for his
mother never threw anything away and the older she
grew the more she filled her life with things, needed or
unnecessary, until it was woven together like a magpie's
nest, and it was practically impossible to find anything
in that abundance of possessions. He would be busy for

ages sorting out her things: paintings and etchings collected by his father; his books, the jewels he bought for his wife, although she seldom wore any, and then the more personal possessions, the letters, photograph-albums and scrap-books with which she had surrounded herself all those years in an alien land. Perhaps he should rather have stayed and studied those discoloured photographs and cuttings, George thought; perhaps from them he would have learned more than in this strange and remote land among people who spoke the same language as he did but with whom he had nothing else in common.

The house was old and over the years succeeding generations had obviously added what they needed, so that one uninhabited room followed on another and often a passage led him astray or a staircase led him higher into clammy darkness. He heard a sound on the roof and fine plaster drifted down. He could no longer see the wall in front of him; his hand touched a doorknob and he entered a room. A young man turned around swiftly and remained standing against the wall opposite him, ready, it seemed, to defend himself.

It was a moment, frightened and surprised as they were, before they recognized one another. The young man whom he had disturbed here was one of those he had met yesterday in the kitchen, dressed in khaki, his broad face expressionless.

'What do you want?' he asked.

'Your mother said I could look around the house.' Was Mrs Hattingh his mother? No-one had said so.

'Are you looking for anything?'

'No, I'm just looking.'

The young man stared at him, hostile and alert, as if

still prepared to defend himself at any moment against an attack. Without a word, George turned and walked away. In the passage he paused until his eyes became accustomed to the dark, and it was quite some time before he heard the young man move again.

The day darkened, the sky was sombre. 'It's going to rain, said Mrs Hattingh again while she shuffled back and forth laying the table. 'Perhaps my husband and the others will come home to eat.'

'They won't come,' said the girl. 'It's not raining yet.'

'When they see that it's going to rain, perhaps they'll come.'

'They won't come. If it rains they'll shelter in the truck. They've got bread and coffee with them: Johannes brought them coffee.'

The girl took part in the conversation absently, from where she was standing in front of the window. 'Come and eat,' Mrs Hattingh said to her. Inside it had grown so dim that only the oil-cloth on the table still glimmered.

'It's a simple meal,' said Mrs Hattingh to George. 'At this time of the day we eat very simply.'

'It's good enough.' The girl was impatient. 'It's not necessary to apologise for everything.'

'You don't know any better,' said Mrs Hattingh angrily. 'You grew up when things were as they are now and you've never known anything better. I'm not used to giving guests bread and coffee for lunch.'

'It's time you got used to it: we've lived like this long

enough.'

Mrs Hattingh didn't pursue the matter. 'I've opened a jar of jam,' she said to George. The girl drank her coffee, said nothing more to them, and didn't eat the jam.

The wind grew stronger and tugged at his shirt as he walked across the yard after the meal. Rain was close, but he chose to go out and escape from the silent house. The long grass rippled, the wind tore at the trees and hurled the first scattered rain-drops against his face. Then the rain fell heavily and he just reached the shelter of a shed in time.

The yard was transformed into a foaming sheet of water and gusts of rain blew in through the open door. It would last for a long time, he realized, and began aimlessly investigating the shed, but it was abandoned: there was only mouldering straw, dried corn-cobs, and empty bins. He went to sit on a wooden crate, waiting for the rain to end, and things gradually became visible in the half-light: a harness hanging against a wall, a ladder leading to the loft and a motionless dark shadow above, which slowly took shape and he realized there was a person sitting there looking at him.

For a while they sat motionless. George heard water from a leaking gutter dripping monotonously near him. Was it the girl or one of the men, he wondered, and why didn't he speak?

'Can you see in the dark?' George called up eventually to the loft.

There was no response and for a moment he thought he had mistaken bales or sacks for a person. But then someone moved opposite him, laughing softly.

'I have nine lives, also,' he called back.

It was a man's voice. George stood up and walked

towards him. 'How long have you been sitting there?'

'Oh ages, even before the rain started. You didn't see me, did you?'

'Can I come up?'

'If you won't tell anyone that you found me here.'

George climbed up the ladder to the darkness of the loft. 'Shouldn't you be here?' he asked.

'I should actually be sorting potatoes in the store-room. But when Johannes went off to the fields, I dodged in here.'

'Why?'

For a while there was no answer. 'I saw you walking past and I expected you to take shelter here. You didn't see me, did you?' he asked again and laughed as if it were an achievement of which he was proud. George couldn't see his face clearly but the voice was that of a young man.

They listened in silence to the drumming of the rain on the corrugated iron above them. 'Where were you going to when you walked past here?' the boy asked.

'I was just walking around, looking at the farm.'

'And what do you think of it?'

'It's all new to me, interesting.'

'Where do you live?'

'In Switzerland.'

The young man was silent, digesting this fact. 'There are mountains in Switzerland,' he said. 'The Alps.'

'Yes.'

'And cows with bells round their necks. I know — I've read about that. And. . .' He hesitated. 'And the capital is Geneva,' he added, mispronouncing the name.

'No, it's Berne.'

'Are you married?' the young man asked. 'What work

do you do? What sort of house have you got?'

It was the first time anyone here had questioned him about himself and he was a little surprised by the boy's curiosity. 'I'm not married,' he said. 'I have an apartment in Geneva. I work at a publisher's there.'

The young man was silent, apparently waiting to hear more. 'My mother had a villa just outside Lausanne, at the other end of the lake,' George added.

'Tell me about your apartment.'

George hesitated. 'It's on the sixth floor, fairly big — the living-room is large.' The young man waited, listening. 'There's a Berber carpet and books and a few paintings from my father's collection and a big fire-place where I have a fire in winter.' He sought for something else, some other fact to mention. 'In winter we often go up into the mountains to ski,' he added and then couldn't think of anything else to say and his voice died away. All the familiar parts of his life sounded strange and insubstantial as he tried to describe them here, on the hay of a dark loft, the drumming of the rain above his head, to someone opposite him whom he scarcely knew and whose face he could not even see. He could smell sweat and earth, the body-smell of someone who worked on the land. Would this boy know anything of Berber carpets, ski-ing expeditions, villas? Did he even know what the words meant?

'Why do you want to know all about it?' asked George.

The boy jumped up quickly. 'Come with me,' he said.

'Where to?'

'Johannes has gone to the fields again, but if the rain keeps up they may come back and they mustn't find us here.'

High in the wall of the loft there was a door, and with a swift movement his companion pulled himself up to it. 'But you mustn't tell anybody,' he whispered, putting his hand out to help George up.

They were now in a long narrow attic with a steeply-pitched roof, so that they had to walk bent under the ridge, and then, through a barricade of cross-beams and tie-beams they came to a second, wider loft lit by a dormer window. There were chests, and old pictures and framed portraits against the walls; on the floor were newspapers and the yellowing pages of magazines, a few burnt-out candles and a mattress, on which the boy threw himself. 'I lock the door out of the shed behind me, then no-one can find me here,' he explained.

In the light George now recognized one of the young men who had been in the kitchen the previous night, the youngest of the three; he had an alert face and dark eyes. When George looked he saw those eyes fixed on him, almost greedily, but then the boy evaded his glance and didn't look directly at him for some time.

'Why do you want to get away from the others?'

'Why not? To be alone for a while and do as I please.'

'Do what?'

'Anything except what I have to do every day; work on the land, chop wood, sort potatoes.'

'Why do you stay here if you don't like farm life?'

The boy's eyes took in the attic with its roughly-plastered walls and spider-webs. 'One can see that you know nothing about such things,' he said with a slightly superior air. 'It's not as easy as you think.' Then he shrugged his shoulders impatiently. 'I don't want to talk about the farm. Let's forget the farm. I want to talk about anything that has no connection with it, anything that's not here, and what I can't or mayn't do here.' His face clouded over: absently he picked off little bits of plaster and threw them against one of the portraits leaning against the wall.

'Who is that?' said George pointing to the portrait.

'I don't know. Someone's great-grandfather. We've got a lot of stuff left behind by people when they went away.'

'Went where? Where's "away"?'

'Away.'

The glass and the solemn face behind remained unmoved: a bearded man wearing a stiff collar and a frockcoat, and in the background a farm, servants, a long-ago world of horse-and-cart, paraffin lamps, church-going and Bible reading.

The boy laughed. 'Do you know that it's the first time I've ever spoken to someone from overseas, someone who doesn't know all about these things, someone to whom they don't speak for themselves.'

'Don't you ever get visitors?'

'People we know from the farms round about, of course. But they don't count. Or police and government people, agricultural officials and so on.'

'And people from the town?'

The boy's expression remained withdrawn while he went on automatically throwing bits of plaster.

'We seldom go to town.'

'Is it possible to live in such isolation?'

'I don't know. My family thinks it is. But you wouldn't understand,' he added with something that was almost condescension in his voice and of his own accord he changed the subject. 'Look here.'

He dragged a chest away from the wall against which

it had been pushed and George saw that it was a bookcase with improvised shelves. The boy obviously expected him to be surprised or impressed, but it was hard to feign surprise at the sight of a few rows of tattered books.

He had to say something, however. 'What's this?' he asked.

'They're books I collected myself: no-one knows about them.'

The stranger with his secrets and his conspiratorial airs was beginning to make George feel uncomfortable — the boy was after all too old for games like this with secret hiding-places and buried treasure. He could hear the rain diminishing; soon he would be able to make an excuse and leave.

'Why must you hide them?' he asked realizing that he could do nothing but ask questions, for a normal discussion between him and the boy seemed impossible.

'There are books among them we're not allowed to read, banned books. Do you know you could get us all into trouble if you told anyone we had them in the house?'

'Why would I do a thing like that?' George bent down to look at them. It was a diverse collection: plays, historical and political books, volumes of poems, novels. Most of the books were old ones which he remembered seeing in his parents' home. There were a few stray English books amongst the others, and one book was in High Dutch, a Bible history, gilt-edged.

'Are these books banned then?' he asked in a light tone, unwilling to participate any longer in the game.

'They think there are dangerous things in some of them.'

'What sort of things?'

'Subversive things, inflammatory things — I don't know. They don't have to give reasons.'

He glanced without interest through the books. On the fly-leaves he saw names, inscriptions: "Marie, from Daddy and Mummy"; "J. Human, 156 Ninth St"; "Christmas 1947". 'Where do they come from?' he asked.

'Oh, from all over. Some were in the house; some I got myself, some belonged to people who left.'

'Do you read them?'

'Yes, when I'm here on my own.'

He leafed through the books. Some had glossy paper, some the drab austerity paper made in the war, and there were typescripts too, carbon copies worn at the edges. 'Why do you show them to me if it's so risky to have them?'

The boy lay on the mattress, staring at him in the same eager way as before and then once again swiftly looked away. Ill at ease, George began to put the books back in the cupboard.

'I don't know. I've never shown them to anyone. Nobody knows about them. Otherwise there'd be no point.'

'If anyone were to search the house they'd find them soon enough,' George remarked, but the boy lay on his back staring at the ceiling and gave no sign of hearing.

'It's not raining any more,' said George. 'I must go.'

'You won't tell anybody?' the boy asked without stirring.

'No, of course not.' George hesitated momentarily, aware of a feeling that he had failed but he didn't know in what way. What could he have said, what gesture could he have made that would have been adequate? He turned to go.

'Shut the door after you,' called the boy, when George was in the first loft, bending under the beams of the low roof.

It had stopped raining, the clouds had passed over, the day smelled cool and fresh. He walked away from the house along a stony footpath which followed the rising contour of a ridge. Then he stopped and looked back. Behind him he saw the huddled roofs and rough stone walls of the farm, the prickly-pear bushes, fig-trees and the windmill; all around stretched a limitless expanse of veld. Was this what he was seeking? Was this the answer? Was it this his mother had dreamed of, this for which she had longed; was it to this she had, at the end, turned in her bed, arms outstretched, half-stupefied by the sedatives the doctor gave her? An isolated house with trees, a stony foot-path, and a great silence under the vast sky in which clouds floated past, drifted away?

Someone was approaching from the other side of the ridge with a few cows. He recognized Hattingh, and waited for him.

'So,' said Hattingh as he came up. 'I went to fetch the cows from the paddock. It was a good rainfall, eh? It's been another good year, thanks be to God. Sometimes we manage by the skin of our teeth, we just get enough for survival, but this year was better.'

'Is it only you and your family who live here?' asked George.

Hattingh gave him a sharp look. 'Why do you ask?'

'It must be difficult to keep such a big farm going?'

The slight, almost indiscernible tension passed. 'We've lost most of our land: they expropriated it, and we had to sell part of what was left for an experimental farm once — we'd had a difficult year. But there's more left than we can look after.' The cows knew the way home and had gone ahead.

'Does it pay to farm a place like this?'

'It's difficult, but what else must we do? Here we can at least enjoy some independence. We get enough to live on; we lead our own lives among our own people; we're more or less left in peace. . .'

Together they walked on after the cows. 'Have you seen the churchyard?' Hattingh asked. George hadn't realized that there was a little cemetery concealed behind the stone wall alongside the path. 'We don't use it any more, but most of our family was buried here, up to my grandfather's time.' There were a few gravestones with crudely-chiselled inscriptions surrounded by raked earth. 'We keep it in order: it's the least one can do. So little of the past has survived: the graves, the house, a few old portraits. . . Even our family Bible has disappeared. It was an eighteenth-century Bible with a lock, a family heirloom, a valuable thing. When I was little I always longed to be big enough to pick it up. But it disappeared, everything disappeared, before our eyes you might say.'

They stood for a while by the low wall and looked at the graves. The clouds had vanished; the sun, already low in the west, slipped lower and poured light over the farmyard, the drab walls and roofs of the farm-buildings and the cemetery. Then they walked on.

'Perhaps we can have a fire tonight,' Mrs Hattingh said, looking questioningly at her husband.

'How will we have enough wood for the winter if we start making fires now?' said the oldest of the young men. They must be brothers, George thought and once more observed the resemblance between them as they sat side by side at the table. But now he could see the differences too. Johannes was the only one of the three whose name he had established, for it was Johannes who had started up at his entrance that morning in the outside room and who had taken coffee to his father and brother where they were working in the fields. He had the same face as his brothers, the forehead broad, the eyes wide apart; it would have been a pleasant, even an attractive face were it not for the unvarying seriousness which marked it and which had already engraved lines around the eyes and the mouth: watchfulness was like a mask upon it. 'There are still corn-cobs in the shed,' he said thoughtfully.

In the feature of the eldest brother there was no trace of delicacy: his eyes were pale, his movements slow. His face was itself a mask, and one felt that there was nothing behind its lack of expression.

'And how long do you think corn-cobs will burn?' he asked mockingly while he chewed his food.

'For a while, anyway, if we have to have a fire.'

'No-one said we have to have a fire.'

'Why do we collect firewood and save corn-cobs if we can never make a fire?' It was the third brother who spoke, the boy of the loft and the books.

George looked from one to the other while they sat and ate, noting resemblances and differences. Yes, the third was the youngest and no mask yet concealed his face: he spoke without weighing his words, his eyes moved around the room with less wariness.

'We have to save what can be burned until we really need a fire.'

'You people want to hoard everything — nails, tins, old tyres. . .'

'One day you too might find them useful.'

'There was one winter just before we came to live here when we had to use some of the furniture to make a fire,' said Mrs Hattingh to George as if she had forgotten suggesting the fire. George knew that the fire had been proposed for his sake and was embarrassed by the long discussion it had elicited.

'We've certainly got enough firewood to have a fire for an hour or so without getting into difficulties this winter,' said Hattingh. 'Besides, this evening we have a guest.'

This was the refrain of everything he and his wife said, the justification for every deviation from routine. While the young people kept aloof, giving no sign of what they thought or felt, it was clear that George's presence was an exceptional event to their parents. At the end of the meal Mrs Hattingh put the cake she had baked on the table and sent the younger brother to get firewood. Hattingh persuaded George to have a glass of brandy. He poured it carefully for all five men, with an air of excitement as if it marked a special occasion. The boy drank with small, almost reluctant sips; Johannes downed his at a gulp and wiped his mouth on the back of his hand. In the corner to which he had retreated after the meal, the eldest son sat, elbows on his knees, his glass held in both hands, taking no further part in the discussion.

Hattingh became more talkative with drink and convivially took George's arm to lead him to the room where the fire was being made. 'We hardly ever sit in the parlour,' explained Mrs Hattingh, followed them. 'It's so convenient to live in the kitchen. . .' She straightened an ornament and hastily wiped the table top with her apron.

'It's musty in here,' said the boy who was kneeling in front of the hearth laying the fire. 'And damp. You'll have to have a fire all night before this room gets warm.'

'I don't know why you always have to be contrary,' said Mrs Hattingh. The other two boys had followed them, glasses in hand, and now stood in the doorway looking at them.

'It'll take all night before Paul gets that fire to burn,' Johannes remarked. So this was Paul, thought George, the boy from the loft, who now flushed and looked up swiftly from what he was doing.

'If you can do it so well why don't you do it? Always finding fault with others. . .'

'It's not me who wants a fire, so don't try to shove your work on to me.'

'Loudmouth.'

'Quiet now, you two' said Hattingh, and pushed the chairs for himself and George nearer to the fire. 'Yes, it's a hard life, one's always busy. We have very little time to relax and be sociable.'

'It's not like it used to be,' said his wife. 'Sometimes months go by without our seeing even the neighbours.'

'But who's left in the district? The Lubbes have gone, the Visagies gone; Fisantkraal has been expropriated; Rietvlei has been abandoned for years, Heuningkloof's a government experimental farm — they've even changed the name. It was one of the oldest farms in the district, a show-place. . .'

'Heuningkloof and Rietvlei,' said his wife. 'They were lovely places, your father always said.' George was listening to a discussion between Paul and Johannes, to the slow monotony of Johannes's teasing, as the fire began to burn smokily, and his brother's vehement replies. He caught phrases: 'Some of us. . .', he heard indistinctly; '. . .better late than never. . .' Johannes was standing, legs apart, with his empty glass still in his hand and a contented smile on his face. The older brother, too, smiled in the background, the three of them busy pursuing some old quarrel which George couldn't follow. 'You have to start at the bottom,' Johannes said smiling. 'If you can't even make a fire you can't do a man's work either.'

'What do you call man's work?' said Paul.

'Things that boys like you have only heard talk about when you've stayed up too late.' He seemed to enjoy trying to anger Paul.

'When I see how you struggle to make a little fire, I wouldn't want to be around when you try to light a fuse,' said the older brother breaking his silence suddenly, and Paul was about to answer when they became aware that George was listening to their discussion. Johannes turned away; Paul bent over the fire again.

'What's the difficulty, Paul?' asked Hattingh. 'Come, let me help you.'

At his intervention the first flame sprang up between the kindling and branches. 'Bring your chairs nearer,' said Hattingh. The three young men remained, however, at a distance, their faces lit by the glow of the fire in the darkness of the room.

'But he was an honest man,' Hattingh went on, continuing his conversation with George. 'Even his opponents had to acknowledge that. He won his court cases honourably, without dirty tricks; he thought clearly and spoke well.'

'He was a Member of Parliament in his time, wasn't he?' asked Mrs Hattingh.

'No, that was Klasie. They tried to persuade Herman to stand for Parliament but nothing ever came of it.'

'Liesbet was against it, of course. Her health was not too good even then. . .'

Suddenly they were silent; they had nothing more to say. The flames crackled among the stumps; outside the wind had risen, making the windows rattle and soot fall from the chimney. They sat in a semi-circle in the dark, staring at the flames. Klasie and Herman and Liesbet were all dead, blotted out, forgotten, except in the memory of the Hattinghs here in front of the fire; dead like his mother and his father before her, with a church full of eminent people; dead like his grandparents. He looked up and in the light of the fire saw Johannes's eyes on him, and Paul silently staring at him. Both looked away, betraying nothing of what their gaze had sought or found.

'Uncle Klasie was at my father's funeral,' said George.

'Yes, he got away in good time.'

'Your parents had been away a long time too,' said Mrs Hattingh suddenly.

'Abroad, do you mean? My father was sent overseas when I was five years old, and they never came back.'

'It must have been hard to live in a strange place, far from your own country and your own people.'

'He was used to it: he was in the diplomatic corps all his life.'

'But in those days he could still have come back if he'd wanted to. Not to be able to return — that must have been hard.'

'Not harder than life would have been for him here,' George answered and realized too late that the remark was tactless.

'I don't know,' said Hattingh. 'Sometimes I think that longing must be harder to bear than any injustice or hardship. If things are difficult you can always convince yourself that you can do something to improve your situation, but what can you do about your feelings? And longing for home above all — this country is part of us: how can we exist without it?'

A log fell in the hearth: they looked in silence at the sparks shooting up.

'I don't know about my father,' said George, 'but my mother suffered great home-sickness.' He remembered the church, the young minister who had come from elsewhere to conduct the service, and how his mother had sat next to him, veiled, with a handkerchief crumpled in her hand. After the service and the interment she stood next to him with the same impassivity while the mourners came to shake hands and say a few words. '. . .a real loss. . .', '. . .a great intellect. . .', '. . .an exceptionally gifted man. . .', '. . .one of the best. . .', '. . .a great loss. . .' After all her years as a diplomat's wife she knew how to stand and shake hands, to remember names and faces, to exchange courtesies without revealing what she actually felt. Many of the people there were not known to him but she remembered them all, and during the drive back to town she told him their names, the ministers, generals, ambassadors, rectors, senators; the men in their uniform dark suits, the overdressed women. Was it only to keep herself from having to think that she had gone on talking? Usually they didn't have much to say to one another; there were seldom moments of intimacy between them.

'My mother had a great longing for this country,' he repeated, looking at the whirling sparks but hearing the tyres hissing on wet tarmac, remembering November, a day of fine misty rain, with pine-trees black against the grey. They passed houses, gleaming plate-glass, placards on hoardings, odd words catching his eye as he looked out, listening to the self-controlled voice of a diplomat's wife making conversation. 'He farmed in our district,' she said. 'You wouldn't remember, but Heuningkloof was a lovely old farm. The last time we visited your grandfather, Granny and I drove over one day to visit Liesbet — she was Klasie's sister-in-law, Herman's wife. She was ill, she was always ill, as long as I can remember. We took you with us with young Mieta to look after you and you ran away from her and hid among the quince-trees near the dam.'

He heard her voice above the murmur of the tyres and saw a policeman waving them on, women with headscarves and odd disjointed words: *Epicerie, Cinzano, Chantier interdit...* He didn't remember the visit she spoke of, neither the afternoon nor the quince-trees.

Then he had turned around and looked at his mother,

sitting upright next to him in the mourner's car, still veiled, and he saw her with unusual clarity. She had always been a stranger to him, a figure at a distance, speaking French or English to visitors or dressing for some dinner or reception, while he himself remained on the fringes of her too full, too busy life, handed over to the care of expensive children's nurses and exclusive boarding-schools. Their meetings were matters of chance, their conversations superficial, the relationship between them barely more than a formality. But he had always accepted these things as natural, without thinking about them. Now, as he turned around in the mourning car and looked at her in the middle of a sentence, of a word, in the middle of the story she was telling, he saw her as if for the first time: a middle-aged woman who had grown up in another country and lived here as an exile, someone whose associations and recollections he could not share, someone with whom he had scarcely anything in common. These links with the past, these elderly generals and Members of Parliament, these were reality for her, he thought, and then realized what his father's death must have meant to her, how great her subsequent isolation would be, left alone in a strange world with half her life lost; then he had put his hand on hers and she had pressed it, bowed her head and wept.

The sparks flew up and disappeared in the darkness of the chimney. 'I can well believe it,' said Mrs Hattingh. 'And then to be left alone: of course she still had you, but your father's death must have been a great loss. She didn't have an easy life either. . .' She was silent and hesitated, reluctant to probe further.

'Luckily she had no financial problems,' said George. 'My father made adequate provision for her and she had a house and a secure income. . .'

'I can't imagine that Anna could ever have been at home in a foreign country,' said Hattingh. 'I knew her well when we were children — it's true it was a long time ago, but after all people don't change all that much.'

George waited for him to continue, but he was silent for a while. 'She had a strong personality,' he added. 'She was always busy with something; she always had to have people about her... Yes, Anna always took the lead in our games: even we boys listened to her.' He began to fill his pipe, busy with his thoughts while he spoke. 'I still remember when she once fell from the windmill at Rietvlei: she must have been nine, ten years old. By rights she should have been killed, but she got off with a few bruises.' He laughed at the recollection.

'And later, when she was older?' George asked.

'Agh, you lose contact with people as you grow up. I went to boarding-school and Anna was away, and later she went to University so we saw one another only in the holidays. She was a pretty girl, attractive. . .' He bent to light a twig for his pipe and spoke no more.

'Did you live with her?' asked Mrs Hattingh tranquilly, her hands folded.

'I live in the city, in Geneva — I work there. My father bought a house for them years ago on the other side of the lake, and after his death she went on living there.'

'She must have been lonely.'

'She didn't want to sell the house although it was really too big for her and too isolated. She had a good house-keeper, but there were difficulties when she became ill. We had to have a nurse for her and they couldn't always get the doctor in time . . .'

'It must have been hard,' said Mrs Hattingh and stared into the fire. It meant nothing to her, he saw, and in fact she asked him no more questions. The questions put to him in this house all related to the known, the familiar, but the slender middle-aged invalid on the rose-coloured divan with her French magazines and English novels afforded them no links. In the silence broken only by the crackling of the fire, it was possible to steer the conversation in a new direction and touch on other topics, but he wanted to talk about his mother and hear more of what they could tell him about her.

'She lived very quietly after my father's death,' he said. 'It wasn't necessary to entertain so much, of course; many of their guests had been his professional acquaintances. And it wasn't long after his death that she fell ill.' They were barely listening; there was no response. 'She went to London and Paris a few times,' he said. 'She was fond of opera and ballet. Once she went on holiday to the Italian lakes but she became ill there and she had to come home after a week. She went with a friend,' he added in a last effort to win their attention. 'Mrs Minnaar; her husband was military attaché . . .'

His effort was fruitless: they sat in their semicircle looking at the flames as if they'd forgotten his presence. His voice died away and he looked at their motionless faces in the light of the fire, his eyes moving from one to another, and then he saw that the girl who had stayed behind in the kitchen had come in unobserved and was standing behind the others, looking at him. He could just make her out on the edge of the group, and he wondered when she had come in and how long she had been standing there.

The oldest son yawned and stretched. 'I'm going to

bed,' he said. 'I'm sleepy.'

'Why are you so unsociable?' asked Mrs Hattingh reproachfully.

'I've got to get up the same time as usual: there's lots of work.' ·

'We must take the potatoes to the Co-op,' said Hattingh.

'Surely not tomorrow?'

'Tomorrow or the day after. We can't wait until next week.'

Johannes also pushed his chair back. The three young men had taken no part in the conversation, talking only among themselves, but when they rose the group nevertheless broke up.

'Yes, I suppose it's time for bed,' said Mrs Hattingh. She sighed, but remained seated.

'Do you still intend to drive over to Rietvlei tomorrow?' Hattingh asked George.

'If you can tell me how to get there.'

'Oh it's not difficult, but it seems to me scarcely worth the effort of going all that way. There's hardly anything left, the buildings were completely destroyed.'

'By whom?'

'It's been neglected for years; not a soul ever goes near there. The whole farm has run wild. You people have waited too long.'

'There must be a caretaker. They told us there was a caretaker — my parents sent money regularly . . .'

Hattingh laughed. 'Someone's cheated you nicely. They enjoy it, they're only too pleased if they can get something from us. You've got to be on your toes in this country, I'm telling you.'

Mrs Hattingh had looked up when they began talking

about Rietvlei. 'My husband says that I could perhaps drive with you to Moedersgift.'

'Yes of course, Mrs Hattingh.'

'It's months since I've been to see Aunt Miemie, and it's not out of your way to drive past the farm.'

'But I'll see you tomorrow morning in any case,' said Hattingh.

By now they were all standing. Chairs were put back in their places, Hattingh knocked out his pipe, the girl was collecting the empty glasses.

'Have you enough blankets?' Mrs Hattingh asked again. 'I can get you more if you like. The nights are already cold . . .' She pulled her cardigan closer around her while she walked with him to his room, so familiar with the house that she didn't even notice the dark, although he had to feel his way with his hand on the wall. 'Yes, and Aunt Miemie would never forgive me if I didn't take you there: Moedersgift borders on Rietvlei. She and your grandparents were neighbours; she's known your family for years. Last time I was there she spoke about your mother.'

He stumbled and put out a hand to stop himself falling, but she had already reached the door of his room and switched on the light. 'She's a wonderful woman for her age, especially when one considers what she's been through. Her husband was a Senator in the old days,' she added abstractedly and looked swiftly around to see that everything in the room was in order: the old-fashioned bedstead, the wash-stand with its cracked marble top, the cheap wardrobe with a door which didn't close properly and the floral curtains.

'You must say if there's anything you need, George. I may call you by your name mayn't I? After all you're not a stranger. Sleep well, George.'

The night was indeed cold, and this unheated, unused room felt damp. He should have driven to Rietvlei that morning, he though impatiently as he began to undress, and left this place. He would have been more comfortable in an hotel than in this house, and no more of a stranger there than with these people. But where should he have gone? He switched off the lights and got into bed.

It was a dream which recurred regularly, the details always the same although the way he experienced them changed. Was it memory or fantasy, this delicate, colourless landscape over which light drifted; was this coast created by his imagination or was it the North Sea beach of one of his childhood holidays, years ago? He didn't know and he could no longer ask his parents if the place really existed. There was just, every time, the same deserted beach over which he ran under the same lofty sky towards the same broad sea. He turned around and saw, far behind him, people on the beach, figures barely distinguishable in the distance, and he walked on, ran on to where the sea closed over his feet. He heard the booming of the waves, the sound of the wind, the calling of women behind him, but when he turned to go back he could no longer see them. Where had they gone, behind the low line of the dunes, out of sight in the distance, dissolved in the clear colourless light? He walked back, leaving the sea behind him, ran, stumbling in the soft sand of the dunes, and couldn't find them.

It was Mrs Hattingh who woke him. 'I thought I'd bring you a cup of coffee in bed,' she said. 'It's another gloomy morning, I'm afraid.'

Lying in bed, he heard a door slam, a voice somewhere down the passage, muted and unrecognizable, and the wind, which gently stirred the curtains although the window was closed. As a child, he must have lain in bed like this, half awake and half asleep and listened to voices talking the same language, in a similar house, in this very country, but he could no longer remember any of it. His youth was forgotten, his parents dead; he was here only on a visit.

Mrs Hattingh had put on a flowered dress, clearly her best, a relic of a bygone world and a bygone fashion, and she hummed to herself while she prepared breakfast for George.

'I though perhaps Carla could go with us,' she ventured a little uncertainly, although nothing more about Rietvlei or Moedersgift had yet been said.

'Of course, Mrs Hattingh.' He assumed she was referring to the girl with the close-cropped hair who had stared at him in the firelight the night before.

The other members of the family had apparently eaten already and left the house, and he had also nearly finished breakfast when he heard a car outside and Hattingh came in.

'Well, George, did you have a good night? I wish I were you — I was already up before dawn.'

Mrs Hattingh poured coffee for her husband. 'George says Carla can drive with us, Daddy. I think it's a good idea if she comes along to visit Aunt Miemie.'

'Yes, that's fine,' said her husband. Then the girl herself came in and went to sit at the other end of the table.

'George says you can drive with us to Moedersgift,' Mrs Hattingh informed her while she poured coffee but she was obviously uncertain about what reaction she would get. The girl looked fleetingly at George, half indignantly and half in reproach, and then spoke to her father.

'I have to work in the vegetable garden,' she said.

'It's not so urgent. It'd be better if you went with your mother.'

She was silent and stared frowning at the cup in front of her. After a while Johannes came in, and then the oldest brother. They both nodded at George without saying anything and went to sit next to the girl, and once more Mrs Hattingh went to fetch the coffee-pot.

'If my wife and the others are going with you there's no need for me to explain to you how to get to Moedersgift,' Hattingh said to George, 'and it's easy enough to get to Rietvlei from there. I hope it won't disappoint you. But as I said, if I were you I wouldn't take the trouble to go there.' He drank his coffee, took his hat and went out.

'Who else is driving to Moedersgift?' asked Johannes.

'Only Carla and me,' said Mrs Hattingh.

'Why are you on again about my going along?' The girl turned on her mother, speaking quickly in a low voice, as if she had only been waiting for her father to leave.

'You can't stay here on the farm like this, day in and day out.'

'Why not?'

'Just look at your hands.' Mrs Hattingh spoke heatedly.

'What's wrong with them? The work's got to be done after all. What must I go to Aunt Miemie's for? I don't want to sit and drink coffee and listen to all her complaints.'

'You must get out among people for a while. When I was your age . . .'

'That's quite a different matter.'

'In any case, your father said you could come — that you must come,' she corrected herself. 'I don't know what George will think of your being so difficult, especially after he's said you can drive with us.' Their conversation was conducted in such low voices that he could barely follow it.

'Who's going with Ma?' asked Paul who had just come in.

'Carla,' said Mrs Hattingh abstractedly, and put out a cup for him.

'Now listen to him whining,' said Johannes.

'Why can Carla go along?' Paul was indignant.

'Because your father said so.'

'Why can't I also go? I also want to go to Moedersgift.'

'What did I tell you?' asked Johannes.

'Why can't Paul rather go instead of me?' asked Carla. 'If there's anyone who actually wants to visit old Aunt Miemie . . .?'

'Who's said anything about wanting to visit Aunt Miemie?' asked Johannes. 'He doesn't even know why he wants to go: he just can't bear it if anyone does something he can't do.'

'Oh, stop it,' said Paul.

'And Carla on the other hand can't bear to be told what she must do,' continued Johannes undisturbed, smiling, his elbows on the table. 'Then she digs her heels in, haven't you discovered that yet? Rather tell her that she can't go to Moedersgift, then she'll walk all the way just to visit Aunt Miemie.'

'Oh shut up!' Carla was impatient.

'Paul wants to visit Bettie!' cried the eldest brother suddenly as if he had just made a discovery, and Johannes laughed.

'Carla, go and get ready,' said Mrs Hattingh. 'I'm sure George will want to leave soon.'

'He's already let Pretty Bettie know that he's coming,' said the other brother.

'Look, he's even combed his hair today!' Johannes chimed in.

'Leave me alone,' said Paul sullenly.

'Is the visit for Bettie, Pretty Bettie Conradie? Or for Fanie? Are you going to read poems with Fanie by the river?'

'Oh leave him alone, Johannes,' said Carla.

'What's it for then? You've been all excitement since you heard yesterday that there was to be a drive.'

'Now that's enough, Johannes,' said Mrs Hattingh, but he went on, grinning across the table. Paul reddened and looked as if he was going to lose his temper, but it was Carla who responded, and with a swift unexpected movement she grabbed the bread-knife and hurled it towards Johannes so that it stuck fast, quivering, in the table in front of him. He leapt up but Mrs Hattingh was already beside him pushing his hat into his hands. 'That's enough now. Off to the fields, both of you.' She was breathless with tension as she pushed him towards the door. The other brother followed, laughing. 'And as for you, Carla, go and get ready at once. I don't want to hear another word.'

The girl stood up and went out as calmly as if nothing had happened, and only Paul remained behind in the kitchen.

'Can I drive with you to Moedersgift?' he asked.

'I've no objection,' said George and Paul smiled at him, a private smile, like that of a fellow-conspirator, before he too left the kitchen.

'These children of mine, I don't know what you must think of them,' Mrs Hattingh said, flustered and apologetic. She started to roll up her sleeves, remembered that she was wearing her good dress, and picked up her apron from the back of a chair where she'd left it. 'They look placid but one just has to anger them and they're devils. Paul, especially, gets furious in a second, so of course they're always teasing him. He just can't hide his feelings, he's still a child really.' With jerky movements she collected the cups and wiped the table. 'Carla's difficult too. As a child she was already quick-tempered; and obstinate! Nothing could ever make her change her mind. But what sort of life is this for a girl on the farm?' she asked with sudden bitterness. 'Busy chopping wood and hauling sacks of fodder like the men. How can one grow up like that?' Her hands were still shaking as she carried the cups away, the question unanswered.

Carla hadn't changed her clothes: she came out in her customary khaki shirt and trousers. Her mother seemed to be about to say something but kept quiet.

The day was overcast, the earth patchy with sunlight and shadow. The road was uneven, muddy, overgrown with weeds, and on either side of them stretched the bleached desolation of the veld. Sometimes for a while a rusty barbed-wire fence ran alongside the road; sometimes it was possible to make out the remains of long-neglected fields swallowed up by grass, or a clump of overgrown trees, relics of orchards among the thornbushes, and then the veld took over again.

'This is Botha's Drift,' Mrs Hattingh said as she sat in front next to George, her voice breaking the silence, and he saw a wall of chiselled stone which had once served as an entrance to the farm, but there was no gate, and rubble had been piled up in the opening to obstruct entry. Mrs Hattingh didn't look at it nor add anything. 'Here you must turn left,' she said and he turned into a road even more neglected than the first, long grass scraping the underside of the car.

'Is it far?' he asked.

'About five kilometres,' said Carla behind him.

'Let's hope the car doesn't break down. I've no tools with me.'

Sitting next to his sister, Paul laughed softly. 'No-one's even brought a gun along,' he said.

Mrs Hattingh turned around. 'Do you mean to tell me—' she began but he interrupted her.

'I thought you'd see to it. After all, you organized this expedition.' He was obviously teasing her, and Carla intervened.

'We hardly need a gun to drive the short distance to Moedersgift, and in daylight at that.'

'Why should we need a gun?' George asked.

Carla looked out again, her head turned away. 'It's safer, but it's not necessary.'

Mrs Hattingh was not reassured. 'Yes, it's easy for you two to talk,' she said reproachfully. 'If you'd been through what I've been through . . .'

Along this road he must have ridden before, with his grandfather. 'You wanted to drive with Grandpa everywhere he went,' his mother once told him. 'When he went to town in the pick-up you sat beside him.' If she hadn't told him he would never have known; he had listened to her words and then forgotten them again, and now, for the first time, he was reminded of them as he returned along the same road towards the same house.

'There's Moedersgift,' said Mrs Hattingh.

Where the veld stretched away before them, he saw in the distance the first signs of human habitation: a few grey buildings, a green vegetable-patch, a windmill and sparsely-scattered trees. As they approached, he could make out other details: a little dam, the flower-garden in front of the house, a calf tethered to a post, a bath-tub overturned against a wall and in the windows faces of children which disappeared rapidly. No-one else appeared, and when he stopped in front of the house and switched off the engine there was once more only silence, enveloping them like the wind.

He saw flowers against a grey wall, a broad verandah, and a front-door which stood open revealing a half-lit passage. In the car, no-one moved.

'The police are waiting for us,' said Paul. 'They've occupied the house and when we get out of the car, they'll open fire from Aunt Miemie's bedroom.'

Mrs Hattingh turned around, a rebuke on her lips, when they heard a voice, the shrill voice of a woman, in the distance. George looked but could see no-one, garden and verandah still deserted while the high-pitched untiring stream of words approached them. Then he saw that someone was coming towards them along a dim passage in the house and gradually, talking all the time, she appeared on the threshold, a scrawny old woman in a shapeless grey frock, her wispy hair cut short; inch by inch she shuffled towards them with the help of two stout sticks while she spoke without pause for breath. ' . . . and you just sit there in the car and you look at me as if it's an everyday affair for you to drive over to Moedersgift!' she said as she came to meet them. 'Oh you rogues, you rogues! And you, you're the worst of all...' With astonishment George realized that she meant him. 'You who gave me such a fright with your strange car here in the road. I know all the cars in the district, all the cars and trucks, but yours I don't know. What's a stranger looking for on the road to Moedersgift if it's not trouble? How was I supposed to know who was with you?'

She spoke without looking at him, almost as if she were unconscious of his presence, and without reproach in her voice. They had climbed out and Mrs Hattingh had already reached her where she was shuffling along the stoep. 'Let me tell you who this is, Aunt Miemie,' she said, but the old woman made an impatient gesture.

'You must be all right, otherwise Mart and her family wouldn't be driving around with you.'

'It's Anna Neethling's son, Aunt Miemie, Uncle George and Aunt Lottie's grandson, from Rietvlei; do you remember?' Excitedly Mrs Hattingh awaited a response.

The old woman withdrew into herself for an instant, considering, and then she looked at him, as if from far away, over a vast distance, screwing up her eyes in the effort to recognize him.

'So,' she said without approval. 'It's a long time since we had a Neethling here as a visitor.'

'He isn't a Neethling himself, Aunt Miemie. He's Anna's son. But his name is also George.'

'I dreamed about George Neethling only last night,'

said Aunt Miemie. 'He was lying in his coffin with a white cap on.' Then she turned from him to the familiar faces. 'Heavens, Carla, but you're growing! It's a long time since I saw you last. And Paul: you're already such a grown-up young fellow. What's the matter with Hennie then, Mart? Why didn't he come too?'

She had begun to turn back to the house, slowly and laboriously, with the help of her sticks, while she asked questions and went on talking without waiting for answers. Mrs Hattingh was still trying to get a word in, but to no avail; she could just walk along, her arm half encircling the old woman while the long shuffling journey was resumed.

George remained on the verandah with Carla and Paul, for there was not much sense in following the women step by step over the threshold into the twilight of the house, and they stood there waiting until Aunt Miemie broke off her monologue to call back to them that they must come in.

It was so dark in the house that for a moment he could see nothing when he entered and was conscious only of the chill and damp which fell upon him, mixed with the strong smell of polish. Only gradually did the dull gleam of linoleum and furniture become visible as he followed the two women along the passage. Curtains were drawn in all the rooms they passed, and it was this that made the house so dark, even darker than it would have been behind the broad verandah in the dull weather.

Somewhere there was the sound of a door slamming and of footsteps, the click of a woman's high heels on the linoleum of the passage.

'I'm sorry, Aunt Miemie,' he heard someone say breathlessly, 'we were busy with the children, I couldn't come sooner. Aunt Mart, I never expected . . .' 'Go and get the sitting-room ready,' Aunt Miemie interrupted, and the heels tapped away from them without George being able to see the woman herself in the half-light. He heard curtains being drawn back and chairs pushed about, and Aunt Miemie continued her journey while Mrs Hattingh listened and nodded and responded from time to time, often cut off in mid-sentence. It was a young woman whose voice he had heard in the passage, he saw, when they finally reached the sitting-room where she stood waiting with folded hands: a thick-set girl in her early twenties, her broad serious face without make-up, her hair twisted into a mass of tight little curls. Did her hair curl naturally like that, he wondered, or was this coiffure her only expression of vanity? He realized that he was staring at her while she and Mrs Hattingh helped to lower Aunt Miemie, still talking, into a chair. 'George,' said Mrs Hattingh, 'this is Bettie Conradie who runs the school here,' and she began to explain who he was. The girl's smile and gesture of welcome were swift and avid, as if this was what she had come for and for which she now stood waiting, and her hand rested limply in his while she listened to what Mrs Hattingh was saying.

'From Switzerland? Oh, how wonderful! You must come and talk to the children: they've often — '

'Bettie, how about coffee?' Aunt Miemie interrupted, and, heels clicking, Bettie disappeared. All the floors in the house were apparently covered with the same gleaming linoleum; they could hear her moving around in another room while they went to sit on the chairs arranged in a semi-circle around Aunt Miemie's uncomfortable arm-chair, so that the old lady remained in the centre of the group. For a moment she was silent, her eyes resting on George.

'George Neethling's son, you said?'

'Grandson, Aunt Miemie.'

'I should have known you were a Neethling even if no-one had told me: you look like them. But not much.'

'Do you still remember Anna?' asked Mrs Hattingh sitting next to the old woman.

''Anna Neethling grew up in front of my eyes — why shouldn't I remember her?'

'She died a few months ago,' said George.

'Time goes quickly,' she said, undisturbed. 'It's nearly twenty years since my husband died. You must be Kosie,' she added disconcertingly.

'Kosie was Anna's brother, Aunt Miemie, George's uncle,' said Mrs Hattingh.

It took a while for her to absorb this. 'And what became of him, then?'

'They took him away, Aunt Miemie. He died in gaol.'

Was that what had happened to Uncle Kosie, thought George, Uncle Kosie who had inexplicably disappeared, the laughing young man in the photograph-albums? Aunt Miemie weighed the information and rejected it.

'Tell me, Mart,' she began, 'have you people already started sowing oats?'

The conversation between the two women was interrupted only when the girl came back with coffee and rusks. The rusks were hard and dry and the cups only half-full; silently they ate and drank while Aunt Miemie and Mrs Hattingh continued their discussion about the farm and acquaintances.

It was chilly here in the sitting-room, and stuffy, the windows closed. It was not surprising that the smell of polish filled the house, he thought, for every surface which could possibly be rubbed shone like a mirror and

floor and furniture reflected the light. Nothing disturbed
that perfect gloss and nothing broke the mathematical
precision with which the room had been arranged, the
chairs an exact distance from one another, the sideboard
against the middle of the wall, the painting of the
Voortrekkers exactly above the middle of the sideboard.
He looked at the vividly-coloured mountain-peaks,
waistcoats and bonnets which contributed the only
brightness to the room and at the portraits of Prime
Ministers, Generals and State Presidents which interrupted
the bareness of the walls at regular intervals. They were all
dead: some borne to the grave, like his father, in wreath-
laden coffins; others dead in obscure and mysterious
circumstances like Uncle Kosie, but death united them in
glory, cold and suffocating like this unused room. Bettie
had withdrawn after serving the coffee and when he
looked around he saw that Carla was no longer in the
room either. She had sat near the door and, silently and
unnoticed, disappeared from her place; only Paul
remained, in the corner, with his legs stretched out in
front of him, not even trying to pretend that he was
listening to the talk of the women. Pretence was hardly
necessary, for Aunt Miemie had forgotten them as she sat
slobbering over her rusk dipped in coffee, interrupting
Mrs Hattingh all the time with a new flow of words.
Energetically, almost angrily, she nodded and the cup she
was holding danced on its saucer. 'Yes, yes,' she agreed,
'it's just the same with me, I sit here all day, I have to sit
here because I can't do anything else and I have to let
other people busy themselves in my house, in my
kitchen . . .'

Engrossed in their conversation, the two women didn't
hear a tap on the window; George looked up and saw

that Carla was standing in the garden, beckoning to him. Even when he stood up the women noticed nothing, nor was there any pause in their talk; only Paul looked questioningly at him as he left the room.

The light of the autumn morning was bright in his eyes after the dusk of the house, and for a moment he stood half-blinded on the verandah before he saw Carla coming towards him between the flower-beds. 'I thought you were probably bored in there,' she said.

'Won't Aunt Miemie mind my disappearing so suddenly?'

'Aunt Miemie hardly knows you're here. She can't grasp new things any more, even Paul and I only just manage to get through to her. Mother's the only one she talks to.'

'She must be very old.

'Oh, she's not all that old,' she said without interest. 'But since the troubles her health's been bad, and her memory's also been affected...' She walked away through the garden, and he hesitated before following her, uncertain whether she wanted his company. It was the first time she had spoken to him.

'Does she stay here alone?'

'The farm wouldn't look like this if she were here alone,' she said a little impatient with his stupidity, indicating the cultivated garden and the weeded yard. 'Bettie lives here with her, and Fanie Raubenheimer, and the children.'

'What children?'

'The school-kids!' Her tone implied that these were obvious things that he ought to know, but then she seemed to take pity on his ignorance. 'There's a little school here on the farm, a sort of boarding-school. Bettie and Fanie run it, and people send their kids here. They board with Aunt Miemie and work for her in the house and on the land. It's considered part of their education.'

'Is it a good school?'

'It's a rotten school but it's our own, and people think highly of Aunt Miemie because her husband was a Senator in the old days: I'm sure Ma's told you already. So they don't mind if their children have to get up at five o'clock to do a bit of work on the farm before school starts.' She gave a short laugh. 'You can get away with anything if you know how.'

The unexpected mockery in her words surprised him. 'Why don't you like her?'

'I never said I didn't like her. I just didn't want to be dragged out to sit and listen to the old woman while there's so much work at home.'

'You say that as if you're blaming me. It's not my fault you had to come.'

'If you hadn't been here with your car, we'd never have come. That's the school,' she said and pointed to a bare rectangular building some distance from the house, on the other side of the barbed wire. That was where he had seen the children in front of the windows, but now there was no-one.

'In what direction is Rietvlei?' he asked.

'Over there,' she said and pointed. The level veld stretching away, the overcast sky, the silence: there was nothing else.

'Is it far?'

'About seven kilometres by road. Why don't you go there since you're so keen?'

'What about your mother?'

'Aunt Miemie will keep her here a few hours still; they

won't miss you. In any case she wouldn't want to go along. There's nothing to see at Rietvlei.'

'How does one get there?'

'Continue along the road — you can probably still see it but it's terribly neglected. It goes only to Rietvlei and it's years since anyone has used it.'

'Are you coming with me?'

'You'd rather go alone.'

'What makes you think so?'

'I don't know. I don't even know why you want to go there. But it's important to you, it's something private, it concerns no-one else.'

'Come with me.'

She hesitated for a moment, and then she walked with him to the car. No-one came out to look as they drove over the yard, and as they turned out of the gate, the windows of house and school remained empty.

The road was neglected, as Carla had said, its course almost lost in the long grass of the veld, so that he had to drive slowly, and it was she who gave him directions when he was in danger of losing the way.

'Have you been to Rietvlei before?' he asked.

'Long ago, when I was little, with my dad, but I don't remember it any more. As long as I can remember, the old people lived in the village.'

He had to concentrate on the road with its stones and potholes, and they were silent. There were no fences partitioning the fields, no remains of orchards or houses. Had he driven here with his grandfather — a man with suntanned skin and clear blue eyes? That much he could remember, that and the old man's pipe and tobacco-pouch. 'The Africans on the farm always had great respect for you grandpa,' his mother had said. What else remained, what except these memories had survived the years? Now even the road there was swallowed up by weeds.

'I don't think we can drive farther,' he said.

'It doesn't matter. The farm is just there, behind the ridge. We can walk.'

They walked on through the tall grass; he stumbled over stones, and branches clawed at his clothing. On the other side of the ridge before him lay, then, the farm and he felt a strange excitement take hold of him. What was he expecting? He didn't know; he was conscious only of a feeling that something would now, at last, be made clear to him; that unformulated questions would be answered and fragmented memories would cohere in a recognizable pattern: his mother's averted head and her hand limp on the bedspread, a voice which made him look up and wonder where he had heard it, a call in the distance, and the slow monotonous clanking of metal in the great silence of a summer afternoon years ago.

He followed Carla up the gentle slope of the ridge and paused for a moment; he saw veld stretching away, slate-coloured hills in the distance, sunlight showing between clouds, and a desolation nowhere interrupted.

'Where is it?' he asked.

'There,' she said' pointing, and walked on. 'I told you there was nothing,' she called back to him. 'Dad told you more than once that there's nothing.'

She walked purposefully, and when he followed her he saw a few stones, trees, shrubs, thorn-bushes. But where was the house, the garden, the stables, the barns?

'Look,' said Carla, 'we told you. Now are you satisfied?'

The buildings must have been here, he realized, here

where he and Carla were standing, but he found only the remains of walls, in the cracks of which weeds had begun to grow, and the outline of old foundations in the grass. Blown away by the wind, washed away by the rain, covered by sand, the relics of that ancient civilization he was seeking; all that remained were scattered stones and fruit-trees which hadn't been pruned for years.

He walked about, looking at what ruins there were. 'What happened to it?' he asked.

'The old people left here ages ago. They couldn't manage the place any longer and they didn't want to stay here alone. So they left and went to live in the town.'

'But not so long ago that everything could just disappear?'

She had gone to sit on a heap of stones while he walked about. 'They blew up the buildings,' she said after a while.

'Who did?' She didn't answer and he walked up to her. 'Who blew them up?'

'Soldiers came to do it. They blew up everything here with dynamite.'

'But why?'

It was some time before she answered. 'Why do you ask so many questions? Couldn't you have rather stayed where you were? Why did you have to come all the way here to ask questions, to ferret things out?'

'It's my family's farm after all: I inherited it from my mother.'

'That's all in the past, all over and done with. Why don't you just forget it? Let the dead bury their dead as it says in the Bible, doesn't it — or do I remember it wrongly? Come, let's go back to Moedersgift.'

She was already on her feet but he didn't move, and

then she looked at him with a direct unwavering gaze. 'Go,' she said. 'You don't belong here after all.'

'But the farm is mine.'

'Sell it, if you can find anyone who still wants it. Otherwise leave it and forget about it. Let the guinea-fowl nest here, let the meercats and rock-rabbits take over. Go back to where you came from.'

He walked away from her and found a broad row of stone steps in the grass, leading from nowhere to nowhere. There had been a verandah here, he remembered, where the daylight filtered through massed plants in pots and tins, his grandmother's plants, and she looked after them and superintended the servant whose task it was to water them daily. He looked up. How did he know that? How did he know how she had stood there among the ferns, a farmer's wife with grey hair, giving the servants instructions? Could he really remember it, had his mother spoken of it, or had the image been preserved somewhere in the photographs of an album? But how was it then that he still remembered her voice, the snip of the scissors as she clipped dead leaves, the sound of coffee-cups?

There were cane chairs which creaked in the heat and people sat here talking in a green shade. Beyond, on the other side of the leafy screen, the garden was dazzling in the fierceness of the sun. You went down the steps and the great lawn stretched before you, bordered by flowers and shrubs, where there was always a garden-boy busy weeding or carrying buckets of water. How was it that after all the years he could still remember his grandmother's voice calling the servants: 'Sagarias!' 'Molefe!' What she had added was inaudible to him now but the sound of her voice was still clear in his memory. Here there had been cannas, he thought, but he found no trace of them among the weeds.

'There was a dam,' Carla said unexpectedly. 'Over there.'

He followed her through the long grass without fully realizing that she had spoken, and she showed him the remains of a wall and muddy ground where water still oozed among stones. There had indeed been a dam where they'd swum, the water full of bobbing, gambolling children and someone had taken a snapshot. 'This one's Elsie,' his mother had said, 'and Martin and Annette; this is one of the neighbours' children — Nettie Prinsloo rode over that day from Botha's Drift to visit. And that's Mieta behind the dam wall, the little maid. She always looked after you when we went to the farm.' The green of the garden and the brilliance of the flowers, the heat, the splashing water and the excited voices of children, peaches in the orchard, fig-trees casting their dense shadow, the coolness of the verandah where the grown-ups sat talking and drinking coffee.

'What's the matter?' Carla said.

'Suddenly there's so much I remember. . .'

'But you were very young when you were last here.'

'Four or five, perhaps. Not more.'

'Can you really still remember so much?'

'Perhaps not. Perhaps I'm only imagining it all, or it's wishful thinking — I don't know.' He looked at the place where the garden had been, at the place where his grandmother had stood, and saw only the veld. 'Of course, my mother told me lots of things. In the last few months before her death she spoke about the farm continually, always about Rietvlei, practically never about any other place where she'd lived.'

'Well, she grew up here after all.'

'I thought I could still find something. I didn't expect that it would all have disappeared.

'So much has disappeared. My parents lost almost everything.'

'But what became of it all? It was a big house, they had possessions, heirlooms, valuable things. . .'

'I don't know. By the time I knew them, they were already living in the town, in a room in someone's back-yard and they didn't have much left.' The subject obviously didn't interest her, and it was only for his sake that she tried to recall other details. 'It was very clean and the old lady always had cakes in a tin for us when we came there. They were very quiet, the old people.'

'They must have been through a lot.'

'No more and no less than anyone else.' She walked away again, but suddenly stood still. 'There are still roses,' she said. 'They're growing quite wild.'

He followed her through what had been the garden; he heard a rustle of some creature alarmed by their approach; a lizard flashed away from a stone. Something in this wilderness had preserved the memory of flower-beds and paths in the midst of strangling weeds, and he saw the unexpected brightness of full-blown roses. The petals drifted from the branches when Carla touched them.

'I believe the old lady was famous for her roses,' she said abstractedly.

'My mother also loved roses. She always had them in the house.'

Tea-roses in the silver vase in front of the window, red roses like these in the Chinese vase on the sideboard, roses floating in a crystal bowl on the table. 'Grandma was well-known for her roses,' she'd said. 'She had a wonderful way with plants. Of course, we had our own bore-hole on the farm: water was never a problem.' She was busy arranging flowers as she spoke and stepped back a little to scrutinize the arrangement. Water oozed away in the muddy ground; the last petals fell from a branch.

'That's all,' said Carla in a tone which made an end to the visit, but he still stood there, unwilling to leave. 'What is it you're looking for?'

He laughed. 'I don't know. I simply feel that there must be something more than just this. It wasn't just this that my mother dreamed about for months, perhaps years; it's not just for this I've come such a long way.'

She laughed too, softly. 'You people with your dreams,' she said mockingly.

'It was a good life.'

'Maybe, but it wasn't proof against reality. The first gust blew it apart.' She pushed the trailing branches of the rose-bushes aside and strode away.

'You know nothing about it,' he called after her. 'You can't judge.'

'I don't know how it was and I don't want to know either. I'm tired of all the dreams and memories; I don't want to live in the past, I don't want to come and grieve over an old overgrown garden. There's work to do, life must go on. I want to go home.'

She walked along the slope down which they had come, back to where they had left the car, but he stayed behind and moved aimlessly about, bending to pick a handful of seed-grass and letting it blow away with the wind, to pick up a handful of soil which he crumbled fine between his fingers. The only sound was the wind, and he was alone among ruins. 'I once nearly let Kosie drown in the dam,' his mother had told him, but he could no longer remember the details. 'Kosie always did what I put him up to, he was frightened of nothing, I could egg him on to do anything. Of course, I was older than he.' She had smiled. It was a rainy autumn afternoon towards the end of her illness: her hand, lying on her lap, was thin; the gold bracelet was too big for her. She didn't have much jewellery, just some heirlooms and a few modern pieces which his father had bought, but for some reason she was attached to this bracelet, and she wore it until the last weeks when it became too heavy for her arm. 'I always preferred playing with the boys to playing with girls,' she had added. 'I was a real tomboy. It seems such a long time ago. . .' With the half-smile still on her lips she had looked around the room and he'd thought that she was looking for a book or handkerchief or wanted to know the time, time for medicine or time for the maid to bring tea.

The lizard crept out on to the stone and sat alert, its gleaming eyes darting about. He must go, he thought, but it was some time before he slowly climbed the slope back to the car where Carla sat waiting, staring ahead of her without taking any notice of him. But when he got in next to her and was about to start the car, she spoke quickly.

'I'm sorry if I was rude.' Before he could say anything, she continued. 'My mother's always complaining that I don't know how to behave, that I'm not a "young lady", and she's right of course. A person can't learn to be ladylike here, not the way things are.'

The gracelessness with which she apologised was somewhat moving. She looked like a boy with her short crop of hair and determined mouth, an embarrassed and awkward young boy.

'There's nothing you need apologise for.'

'You're probably used to better manners.'

'I'm not interested in good manners; I came to see the country, to get to know the people as they are. . .'

'You must be disappointed, then.'

'Do you want a cigarette?' She nodded and took one, and he lit it for her. 'Today's the first day you've spoken to me. Even rudeness is better than silence.'

She flushed. 'You learn to be careful. You can't trust just anybody.'

'Then I must be grateful that you trusted me enough to come here with me.'

'It's not that sort of trust I'm talking about.'

'Tell me,' he said, 'if you came to Rietvlei only when you were very young, how did you know about the roses and the dam?'

She was silent for a long while. 'I came here with my father on a visit when there were still people here. And later I came once or twice after the farm had been abandoned. You can walk here through the veld from our place.'

He looked at her profile, the high forehead, the straight nose and strong chin, and weighed her words.

'You don't trust me, not entirely.'

'Why do you say so?'

'Not one of you trusts me. There are things you don't discuss in front of me, things I mustn't know, whatever they are. . .'

Somehow a kind of intimacy had come into being between them that morning: with no-one else on the farm would he have felt free to speak like this.

'How can you expect us to trust you? You're a stranger, we don't know you.'

'I'm not a stranger: you know who I am and who my people were. I was born here, just like the rest of you, I lived here as a child, my mother came from Rietvlei. . .'

She smiled a little pityingly. 'What difference does it make who your mother was or where you were born? What matters is what you yourself are, and you're certainly not one of us. You come from abroad, your work, your home, your whole life is there. You know nothing about us, we're strangers to you, this country is only a place where you've come for a few days to visit people who happen to speak a language you understand.'

For a while they smoked in silence, and he noticed that the hand which held her cigarette was trembling.

'Why are you so vehement about it?'

'Agh, I'm just being bad-mannered again, I don't know what I'm saying.' She reflected, and then spoke more quickly. 'Perhaps it's just that I'm jealous, or feel badly done by, I don't know what. You people were among those who got away in time — you went somewhere to be safe and now you've come back to see how things have gone with those of us who stayed behind — you with your expensive clothes, your cuff-links, your gold watch. And we. . .' She stubbed out her cigarette jerkily. 'You see how we live, you can guess how we spent all those years; you can still see the signs, the scars. . .'

There was little he could say. 'I'm sorry you feel like that about it,' he began.

'There's nothing for you to be sorry about, it's not your fault. Others were responsible; it's always someone else; we just inherited it. It's time we went back to Moedersgift,' she added abruptly, and during the return journey along the overgrown track she sat in silence beside him as if once more unaware of his presence.

As they approached the farm, they saw Paul standing in front of the house.

'He's cross because we went without him,' Carla said unmoved.

'Where did you go?' he called even before they were out of the car.

'We drove to Rietvlei,' said George. Carla was already walking towards the house.

'Why did you go so suddenly without saying a word? Why did you take Carla along?' His tone was reproachful.

'She showed me the way. I didn't think it would matter if we drove over there quickly.'

'I also wanted to go to Rietvlei.'

'It wasn't worth the trouble. Your father was right: there's nothing to see.'

'I wanted to go along.'

'Why?'

'I've never been there.'

There was no point in continuing the discussion. 'Did your mother ask where we were?'

'They didn't even know you'd gone, they've just gone on talking. At least Aunt Miemie is talking and Mother is listening.' The dissatisfied expression on his face lifted a little. 'Bettie came to look for you,' he added.

'The teacher?'

'She's almost speechless with excitement about the visitor from abroad. She left the children alone, just like that, to run around looking for you.'

'What for?'

'Oh, so that you'd come and talk to them and tell them about Europe. They've never seen anyone from abroad. At least that's what she says. But just look — here's Fanie coming also.' He laughed softly to himself.

Across the yard, from the little school-building, a young man came towards them. 'Raubenheimer,' he called out as he approached and seized George's hand to shake it heartily. 'I saw you arrive but I couldn't leave the children earlier to welcome you. I had Bettie's class as well as my own, you know. But Bettie told me who you were. My word, but I'm pleased to see an Afrikaner from abroad, a lost sheep, eh?' He laughed uproariously.

George stood there with his hand in the stranger's grip, powerless before his enthusiasm and his size. He towered head and shoulders above George and his hands and feet seemed disproportionately large because of his short jacket sleeves and the heavy, sturdy shoes he was wearing. It seemed as if those big hands and feet didn't belong to him, but had an existence independent of hs body. 'We're completely isolated here,' he said. 'We've set up camp in this remote corner of the country; it's only in the outposts that a person can still be free, and we keep the campfires burning, or try to anyway!' Again he laughed loudly and a bit nervously, twisting his shoulders. 'We two must talk, old chap; I'm sure we've got a lot to say to one another. I hope you'll be staying quite a while?' He stooped to look George in the eye, and waited, smiling, for an answer.

'I must go back in a few days' time. I came only for a week, to see the farm, Rietvlei. . .'

The young man seemed distressed. Was it exaggerated politeness, George wondered, or genuine disappointment?

'My word, but I'm sorry to hear that!' he said with an earnestness which sounded excessive. 'When Bettie came and told me you were here. . .'

'Fanie!' someone called from the house. 'Paul!' It was Bettie, who was standing on the verandah beckoning to them. She had perhaps forgotten George's name or was too shy to call him by it, but when he looked around at her she stretched her hands out to him, beaming, to show that he too must come. Raubenheimer drew him a little closer. 'I see Paul's already taken possession of you: well, you're in good hands, he'll show you around and tell you everything. I'm sure he's as delighted as I am that you're here.' Standing at a distance from them, Paul gave no sign of having heard. 'Paul and I are good pals — I can call you "George", can't I: you don't mind?' But Bettie had grown tired of waiting on the verandah and was coming towards them across the yard. Raubenheimer's voice grew ever more insistent: George felt the man's hand on his arm, his breath on his face, and saw suspended above him the great face of the teacher with glinting spectacles. 'It's a hard life; you can see that for yourself. One does what one can, one tries to keep the flame alive. We have the children, a sacred charge, entrusted to us. . .'

His words came so fast and in such confusion that George didn't even try to follow any longer. Meanwhile Bettie approached inexorably, on heels which wobbled under her weight, her dress stretching tightly across her knees as she tripped towards them. 'You must come and drink coffee,' she called. 'What are you talking about? I've already made coffee and we're only waiting for you people; Aunt Miemie has been asking where you are so that we can start.' While she spoke, it was George she was looking at, and her broad unattractive face beamed with friendliness, with hospitality, with benevolence.

'Yes, yes, we're coming.' Raubenheimer guided George past her in the direction of the house. 'It's seldom we get visitors,' he said, resuming their conversation, 'and someone who has come from abroad is exceptional, you can understand how much there is to talk about.' With short, running steps Bettie tried to keep up with them and hear what was being said, and Raubenheimer pushed George all the faster in the direction of the house to get away from her until the verandah was reached and he halted to straighten his jacket. A little out of breath, Bettie caught up with them.

'You disappeared so suddenly,' she said to George. 'I was with the children and when I came outside again, I saw that the car had gone. I thought you'd left already, I wondered whether I'd dreamed it all. . .' She giggled at what she'd said, and bore him off in triumph.

In the sitting-room, Aunt Miemie was still busy talking while Mrs Hattingh listened and nodded, murmuring a few words from time to time. They took their places again in the half-circle of chairs without the old woman even looking in their direction. Bettie brought a tray of coffee and rusks, the cups only half-full, as before, and then she came and sat next to George tugging her skirt down over her knees. On the other side Raubenheimer twisted about awkwardly with his weight first on one side of the chair, then on the other.

'. . . but goodness, what else must a person do, I ask you? It's not a matter of choice after all.' Aunt Miemie's voice shrilled on and it was a little while before George, hypnotised by its monotony, realised that Raubenheimer was leaning towards him, asking something, his words unintelligible. 'And if you sit here like me, day in, day out

— I needn't tell you, Mart, because you know it yourself, you see for yourself I'm chained to this chair. . .'

Raubenheimer was meanwhile repeating his question. 'Do you read poetry?'

'Yes, occasionally.'

The teacher shifted a little nearer on his chair. 'You like poetry?' he asked but at that moment Aunt Miemie unexpectedly stopped talking and his voice was loud in the silence. He reddened.

'What's that you're talking about, Fanie?' Aunt Miemie wanted to know, impatient of interruption.

'Nothing, Aunt Miemie, George and I are just talking a bit about poetry.'

'Well talk then, talk so that we can hear you.'

'We weren't really saying anything, Aunt Miemie.'

The old lady looked at them questioningly for a moment, and then she turned around and resumed her conversation with Mrs Hattingh. Raubenheimer continued to lean forward in George's direction; on the other side, Bettie also shifted nearer to hear what they were saying. Silent, they remained so on either side of him like heraldic supporters, while Aunt Miemie proceeded with her monologue. '. . .but you can understand it yourself, it's not necessary to tell you what it all means to someone of my age, someone who has been through everything I have. I'm telling you, Mart, sometimes I wake in the night. . .' Mrs Hattingh nodded and put in a reassuring word now and then, and then she looked at George and smiled as if telling him not to lose heart. In the stuffy room with its smell of polish it was hard to stay awake while that high monotonous voice went on: his eyes closed, his head dropped forward, and he awoke with a start. On either side of him Raubenheimer and Bettie sat with folded hands, motionless gryphons, lions, unicorns, guarding him.

A ripple passed through the room, an interruption of the old woman's flow of words, a sudden movement he couldn't immediately account for, and it was some seconds before he realized that Aunt Miemie had stood up with Mrs Hattingh supporting her. Next to him Raubenheimer unfolded himself with difficulty from his chair, disentangling arms and legs, bringing hands and feet into view from unexpected places as he rose. Bettie smoothed her dress over her knees, her eyes fixed on the ground and then also stood up. George's foot had gone to sleep, and he pushed his chair back clumsily. They all stood there, motionless and silent as if an audience were over, a rite celebrated, a sacrifice completed, and only the last words of benediction and dismissal still remained to be pronounced.

'Yes,' said Aunt Miemie plaintively 'nothing can last for ever. If you must go Mart, then I suppose you must.' Her silence was full of suppressed reproach.

'We'll come back again soon, Aunt Miemie,' Mrs Hattingh assured her. 'Just as soon as Hennie gets a chance, he'll bring me over to Moedersgift.'

'Yes, yes, when Hennie gets a chance — I know how it goes, I just sit here in the house, day in day out: it's easy enough to forget all about me. I always say —yes, I've told you already, Mart— I always say. . .'

Her tone was still plaintive, but Mrs Hattingh remained standing and the inevitability of their departure was clear. Aunt Miemie's sticks were once again in position; Mrs Hattingh approached to help, and by degrees Aunt Miemie turned herself in the direction of the door and, talking all the while, embarked on the long shuffling walk back to the passage and the verandah. Past George where he remained standing, guarded by Raubenheimer and Bettie, past the chairs in their expectant semi-circle, past the sideboard and the Voortrekkers, past Prime Ministers and State Presidents, and past Paul who had withdrawn again into a corner by the door. Inch by inch her slippered feet moved over the shining linoleum, and for a moment George wondered if she would ever reach the threshold, or whether she would stay there in the middle of the room, shuffling and tapping, so that only the high voice would remain to attest to the passage of time. But then she moved across the threshold and the others waited for him to follow her. In a procession they once more traversed the dark passage, the two women in front, and then George with Raubenheimer and Bettie behind him, while Paul dawdled after them.

The passage was wide enough for only two people to walk abreast and, following the women, George became aware of a wordless competition between Bettie and Raubenheimer behind him. First one appeared next to him, only to be pushed aside by the other: thus in turn they ousted one another in the narrow passage.

'Excuse me,' said Bettie and laughed nervously as she began to push past him but when he tried to stand aside to let her pass, Raubenheimer pressed his broad shoulders between him and the wall so that Bettie was forced to give way and had to be content with following them close at heel.

'Do you read poems?' Raubenheimer repeated in a confidential tone.

'Yes, sometimes,' George answered as he had before. 'I have to read a lot of proofs and manuscripts at work and there's not always time or inclination to read for relaxation.'

'I love poetry,' said Raubenheimer. 'I couldn't live without it. But perhaps you're not interested in literature?'

'I often go to the theatre,' said George in an attempt to satisfy the questioning, expectant face next to his.

'I read plays as well,' Raubenheimer told him. 'Who are your favourite playwrights?'

'Büchner, Anouilh, Schiller. . .' He mentioned the first names which came into his head, without thinking, but Raubenheimer didn't seem to recognize them. He once more had his arm around George's shoulders to increase the feeling of intimacy between them, or perhaps only to keep Bettie at a distance with his elbow, but she slipped around George and determinedly forced an opening for herself with her hips.

'It's a shame you didn't come a few months earlier,' she told him. 'The children put on a play themselves, it was very good. It was all about the Voortrekkers. . .'

Raubenheimer was now forced to walk behind them, but he kept his arm around George's shoulders and hung on to him while he tried to move forward. Suddenly George lost patience with the struggle in the narrow passage, the talk which was made nearly inaudible by the shrillness of Aunt Miemie's voice, the pressure of Bettie's hips and Raubenheimer who was dragging him back in his affectionate grasp. With almost rude violence he pulled himself free of them and drew back so that they could precede him. Hesitating, they looked at one another.

'But I said so only this morning to Bettie,' Aunt Miemie continued. 'Bettie didn't I say so?' She raised her voice and Bettie had to go to her. 'Didn't I tell you this morning. . .'

George was left alone with Raubenheimer, for Paul, uninterested, kept at a distance. With the same questioning, almost pleading expression, the teacher stared at him, waiting for an answer as if their conversation had never been interrupted. George saw the man's spectacles hovering ever nearer and wondered with a feeling akin to panic how he was to free himself from this unsought intensity.

'I also write poems,' said Raubenheimer in the silence, his voice lowered so that no-one else could hear him, and he stood there, his head bent in George's direction, the gleam of his glasses and his heavy breathing the only indications of his presence in the dim light.

It was a confession, George realized by the tone in which the declaration was made, a sign of trust, a precious secret imparted to him, but he was at a loss how to respond.

'Have you published anything yet?' was the only rejoinder he could think of, and as he said it he realized how foolish it was in the circumstances. Raubenheimer responded eagerly however, delighted with encouragement to continue.

'I've been writing for a long time, as long as I've been able to hold a pen, one might say. There are poems with which I've had much success, if I may say so myself, poems which have been highly esteemed. I feel that it's important work I'm doing, you know; it's also a weapon in our struggle, it's something with which to rouse our people and inspire them. . .' The words streamed forth as if he had waited only for George's question to give expression to feelings and emotions suppressed for months, or perhaps years.

'Fanie, where have you got to again?' Aunt Miemie's voice interrupted the unbosoming. Supported by Mrs Hattingh and Bettie she had eventually reached the front door. 'Aren't you going to say goodbye to Mart?'

Raubenheimer was silent and paused only to pull down the sleeves of his jacket before gripping George by the arm and dragging him along the passage. 'But it was wonderful talking to you!' he whispered swiftly.

'Mart's going now,' Aunt Miemie informed everyone. 'We can only hope that it won't be months again before her next visit.' Carla had appeared from the garden, Paul from the house, and the leave-taking began. George put out a hand to Aunt Miemie.

'Yes,' she said, 'you're also an infrequent visitor. But of course you've no reason to come here any more, now that they're both dead. It's a disgrace,' she declared heatedly, 'it's a disgrace how they were treated. They were chased away from here like kaffirs.' Her hand rested in his, small and thin like a bird's claw, and over some great distance she looked at him again. 'But you yourself have also changed. You used to have such a round face, Kosie.'

'It's not Kosie, Aunt Miemie,' Mrs Hattingh tried to explain again, but the old woman wasn't listening.

'You always used to make us laugh such a lot.' Her tone was reproachful. 'But, there it is, these days people don't laugh any more, isn't it so?'

She turned away from him, his presence forgotten. He felt Raubenheimer's limp, clammy hand in his; Bettie touched his fingertips coyly in a farewell greeting. 'We so wanted you to come and talk to the children. We'll just have to tell them that you'll come next time.'

'Yes,' he promised, 'next time,' and then he was once more sitting in the car, and Mrs Hattingh was leaning out to hear Aunt Miemie's last words from where she was standing on the step, supported by her sticks. 'You must see to it that Hennie brings you here himself,' she called. 'I don't know why I never see him these days. You think you can just forget about me, I just sit here and no-one feels obliged to bother about me...' Her voice faded away in the drone of the engine: Mrs Hattingh waved for the last time and closed the window. The grey house, the garden, the school, the windmill, the blue-gum trees were left behind and he had to keep his mind on the road.

'She doesn't look too bad,' said Mrs Hattingh. 'It's marvellous how much energy that women still has, even though she can't do much.' Then she looked at her children behind her. 'And where did you disappear to this time, Carla?'

'George and I drove over to Rietvlei, Ma.'

Mrs Hattingh wasn't satisfied with the reply. 'And where did you come from when we were ready to go?'

'I went to talk to the children.'

'We hadn't even sat down properly when you disappeared. Aunt Miemie hardly set eyes on you the whole time we were there.'

'Aunt Miemie's not interested in us.'

'That's nothing to do with it. It's a question of good manners.'

Carla sat looking out of the window; she apparently didn't intend to answer. Next to her, Paul maintained his aloofness. Mrs Hattingh sighed. 'Well, now I've done my duty again. I feel so guilty about Aunt Miemie but it's so difficult to get away to see her.'

The veld unrolled past them; the last trees of Moedersgift had already disappeared. Before them there was only the overgrown road, the horizon, the sky.

He could leave now: he had done his duty, found the scattered stones among the weeds, seen the water seep away into the earth.

'I think I'd better go now,' he said to Mrs Hattingh at lunch, but she wouldn't hear of it. Her husband wasn't even at home, she objected; what was the hurry? Surely he could stay with them one more night and drive back to town the next morning? In any case, there wasn't even a train that afternoon, she remembered triumphantly. The train left in the morning at eleven or twelve, she wasn't sure of the exact time, but her husband would be able to tell him.

Very well then, he thought, he'd stay. He had barely unpacked; most of his clothes had been left folded in his suitcase, but he'd already been here two days.

The wind made the loose sheets of corrugated iron on an outbuilding clatter; the windows rattled in their frames. In the kitchen the plates and cups from lunch had already been washed and put away and Mrs Hattingh had wiped the oilcloth on the long table clean. He left the house and walked across the yard, past the shed where he had sheltered and had met Paul, but he saw no-one. This afternoon, however, he was glad to be alone; he sought no-one's company. He walked up the hillock, past the little cemetery Hattingh had shown him, and across the veld; found the stony, dried-up course of a little stream and followed it until he felt that this aimless stroll had lasted long enough. He went to sit on a rock on the bank.

He realized that he was tired, exhausted beyond mere

bodily fatigue. The burden had become too great; the weight of past and present, the things he remembered — things he thought he had long forgotten— the long journey, and the experiences of the past few days, the inexorable nature of reality — a whole complex of things which he himself could barely analyse. He stayed there a long time, barely thinking. But he knew it was necessary to consider things carefully, probe, sum up, make a decision. Where, then, to begin? What now? He found no answer: nothing presented itself.

And yet there must be an answer, he thought, somewhat taken aback and uncomprehending; it was indeed time for summing-up and decision, now that all dreams had been realized and what had so long been desired had become actuality. This was, after all, the promised land, possessed by birth and inheritance, the land about which so much had been spoken and dreamed, the object of such endless longing, for which so much had been endured — even exile and death.

He himself had grown up in a small circle of people from the world of politics, the Army, business; people of high rank, well-to-do people who had had the opportunity of transferring their money to foreign banks and removing themselves and their valuables before the last exits were blocked. They were people for whom it was easy to build a new life and succeed in it, acquaintances of his parents whom he still met at recitals and receptions. The women wore jewels, the men spoke about business to one another; there was still money, influence, privilege; things went well with them. And yet their existence was precarious, for they lived in foreign countries and would never find resting-places there. The longing for home remained.

The longing remained, too, among those who had preserved nothing else; their dreams, even a generation later, still centred on this land, this soil, and they took the memory of it with them into the back-rooms and attics of strange cities, struggling with the syllables of alien languages, dragging their luggage from station to bus, from taxi to train. Rain misted over the mountains and fields of the passing landscape and darkness hid strange roofs and spires; footsteps sounded on the uncarpeted · stairs and a key rattled in a lock. There were departures and arrivals, there were meetings and partings, there were moves from room to room, long journeys from town to town; anxious calculations with strange coins and notes; the hoping, the waiting, the empty days of exile, with ever earlier dusk falling over the fields and roofs, hiding everything from view, until nothing remained except the longing and the dream. On the walls of their rooms hung pictures of other landscapes, while darkness veiled the windows.

The longing remained, pitiless, inescapable, and always, it had seemed to him in his youth when he observed the exiles, they had left their trunks half-unpacked in readiness for return. In the entire structure of the lives they had built up in foreign parts only one thing had reality: the land they had once possessed and then lost.

That possession they had accepted as a matter of course without ever reflecting on its value or meaning, and its loss did not force reflection on them. Rather it seemed as if the implications of exile had never completely penetrated their awareness, and they went forward as best they could as if it had never taken place. Somewhere there had indeed been a slight disturbance, a barely perceptible geological shift, just enough to make the glasses tinkle, but they attached no importance to it. The disturbance was temporary, purely temporary, they assured one another; in reality nothing had changed, nothing could possibly change. The great house still awaited them, the servants stood prepared; the desk, the car, the garden awaited their return, the book still open at the page they'd been reading, the cup on the table were they'd set it down. In that motionless silence the dog pricked up its ears, listening for the sound of their footsteps in the distance.

Temporary, nothing more, they repeated with conviction, a brief delay abroad, a short sojourn in foreign lands, while they waited for the signal to return, possibly next month, probably the month after. The years went by and their stay had already lasted for a generation, but still they regarded themselves as visitors, not exiles, still less as citizens of the lands in which they lived. The dream endured, its lustre untarnished, and their existence was a perpetual attempt to deny the pressure of the reality surrounding them, while they remembered and longed and waited for the hour when it would all be over and they would return to the beloved land.

And now he had returned, the first of the generation brought up abroad. Briefly and in passing he had already seen something of the country: he had seen the glow of sunset and the sudden fall of night; he had heard strange, unexplained sounds in the distance. Posters and slogans on the walls in languages he couldn't understand, placards already beginning to peel off; the fierceness of the sun and the heat of the day; massed bunches of flame-coloured flowers, heaps of strange fruit with the rich sweet smell of decay. He had seen the vast anonymous crowds at bus-stops and on station-platforms, heard children at play, men talking among themselves as they came from work. And he had come here, to these his people, to this earth which now belonged to him, this gravel, stone, sand.

There was no answer, he realized: there was life which had to be continued, and perhaps that continuation was in itself somethng like an answer or as near as one would ever get to an answer. For a long time he sat where he was, leaning back and looking at the grass and stones and plants, the names of which were unknown to him. Above him clouds were driven before the wind; the dry grass rustled. He was tired and no longer wanted to think or remember.

Slowly, aimlessly, he walked back to the house along the bank of the stream and then he saw Paul coming from the opposite direction. They walked on towards one another among the stones, and it seemed as if Paul was pretending not to see him, for even when they were close to one another he didn't look up.

'Where are you going?' asked George and then the boy laughed.

'I was looking for you.'

'Why?'

'I wanted to know where you were. I looked everywhere, even in the loft — I thought you might have gone there.'

'And how did you find me here?'

'I just wandered about. I knew I'd find you.' They walked on together. 'Why did you come here?'

'I also just wandered about.'

'There's nothing to look at here.'

'I didn't want to see anything; just to think.'

'What about?' He didn't wait for an answer. 'Why did

you go to Rietvlei this morning without telling anyone?'

'After all that's what I came for, to see Rietvlei.'

'I wanted to go with you.'

George had already climbed the bank of the stream and saw the veld in the evening sunlight which had broken through the clouds, and the house with its outbuildings at a distance in a hollow.

'I want to talk to you,' said Paul behind him and he turned to look at the boy.

'Talk, then: I'm listening.'

'I ask you questions and you don't even answer me.'

'Tell me what you want to know. Tell me what I can do for you.'

Paul's eyes avoided his. 'What did you and Carla talk about?'

'This morning? I hardly know any more. About my grandparents, about the farm as it used to be, about what I still remember of it all.'

'Carla's not even interested.'

'I know. Are you?'

'I wanted to see the place.'

'You still can, any time — it's near enough if you're so keen to go there.'

'No. Now I'll never go.' He spoke with finality. There was nothing more to say on the subject. 'And now you want to leave.'

'There's no reason for me to stay.'

'Not for you.'

'For whom then?'

'For us perhaps. I'm sure you haven't thought about that.' He was moody, his hands in his pockets. 'You just go away, you go on with your life, and we'll stop existing for you the moment you drive off. But you're important to us, don't you know that?'

'You make me feel responsible. And guilty.'

'Talk to me,' said Paul urgently. 'I've already asked you; talk to me, tell me about anything except this.' He gestured in the direction of the farm buildings. 'About anything except the farm and the sheep and the mealies, anything except about getting up early and working hard and being poor; anything except fighting and suffering and being unjustly treated and jails and prison and camps. I don't want to hear about tasks and vocations, about ancestors or heroism or duty or the will of God. I'm sick of all that.' He spoke vehemently, and George looked at his dark face with a sort of pity, but when he began to speak Paul interrupted him. 'Tell me that there is something else. Tell me that another world exists, otherwise there's no point in going on.'

His face was distorted as if he were going to cry, and George put his hand out to touch him, but Paul shook him off with an impatient movement. 'You really are important,' he said in a subdued voice. 'Now you can see for yourself if you don't want to believe me. Look. Gerhard has heard that you're here and he's already come chasing over to see you.' George remained with his hand outstretched. 'Look, there!' Paul was impatient with his lack of comprehension, but then George saw far away a vehicle moving in the direction of the farm. That must be the main road, he thought, and a visitor was coming whom Paul could already recognize at this distance.

'Who is Gerhard?'

Paul laughed. 'You'll find out: it's because of you that he's coming.'

They stood where they were, watching the pick-up truck which was now clearly visible on the road, the windows flashing in the light of the setting sun.

'Are you coming with me to the house? George asked.

'No,' said Paul. 'They mustn't see me with you. You're not to tell them that you found me here.' Without another word he walked off, taking a course away from the house, When George turned, he could no longer even see the boy.

The clouds had drifted apart; the late afternoon sun flooded the earth and in its glow the drab landscape assumed colour, its austerity softened and enriched. He walked across the veld to the farm buildings awaiting him with their roofs and chimneys; he heard the bleating of sheep in the distance and the clanking of buckets: they were busy milking, he thought, although he hardly knew where his certainty came from. Then the wind came at him and in the sudden gust the vanes of the windmill began to revolve; he heard their rhythmic clanging coming from beyond the barn and the sound made him pause, overwhelmed by the intensity of the feeling it evoked. He had heard it before, that sound was one he had known long ago and then forgotten, but now it was borne towards him from the past with the wind. When exactly had he had heard the clanging of the revolving blades as a child, and where? And what were the feelings which now overwhelmed him? Heartache and longing and hope, a whole world waiting to be conquered, safety, security and illusion, and the turning of a windmill in the long silence of a summer's afternoon, in the vast dusk of the summer night. He walked on to the house, astonished at the emotion which possessed him, and it was as if he were coming home.

Someone called him; Hattingh and another man stood by the pick-up truck which had stopped next to his car.

'You've come at just the right time,' called Hattingh. 'Today you'll get to know all our neighbours, it seems to me — here's Gerhard driven over from Kommando Drift.'

The man standing next to Hattingh put out his hand. 'Snyman,' he introduced himself. His grip was powerful, and his grey eyes looked straight into George's.

'Gerhard and his family are our nearest neighbours; they've farmed for years at Kommando Drift. They're one of the oldest families in his district. His mother knew your people well.'

'The Neethlings were one of the leading families here,' said Gerhard. 'Everyone knew them.' He spoke a little formally, not quite sure what tone he should adopt. He was the same age as Hendrik and Johannes, and wore the same faded khaki working-clothes; tanned and blond, he was a handsome man without seeming to be aware of the fact.

'How long have Uncle George and Aunt Lottie been dead now, Gerhard?' said Hattingh. 'We didn't think we would ever see a Neethling in the district again.'

'Broom is a tough shrub, Uncle Hennie. You can't eradicate it so quickly.'

'Is that a reference to my family?' asked George, and Gerhard looked at him for a moment and then decided to laugh.

'You might say so,' he answered. 'Yes, you might say so.'

'He wanted to leave immediately,' said Hattingh, 'but

we couldn't allow that.'

'No, it's a special event, isn't it? When I heard who was here, I felt I had to drive over to see for myself.'

'Who told you?' asked George.

The grey eyes looked directly into his, but once more there was a short hesitation before Gerhard responded. 'Oh, news like that travels fast: it's not something that can be kept secret. But where are Hendrik and the others this evening, Uncle Hennie?'

'They'll be here presently: we were busy with the milking when you came. And Carla is here somewhere too — she's probably helping her mother. Look, there's Aunt Mart already waiting for you.' Mrs Hattingh had appeared at the top of the steps to the kitchen-door looking to where they stood; from a distance she smiled at Gerhard. 'Hendrik! Johannes!' called Hattingh cheerfully. 'And Carla, come on girl, where have you got to? It's not every day that Gerhard comes to visit us!'

They walked towards the house. From the barn Johannes called and waved and came towards them, Hendrik following him; Mrs Hattingh turned to say something to someone in the kitchen, and then Carla appeared behind her in the doorway. Gerhard remained standing against the wall of the house and laughed; he stood facing the setting sun, golden in the unexpected richness of the evening light; he stood strong and young and glowing, while they all came to welcome him. Hattingh had his arm around Gerhard's shoulder, Hendrik and Johannes greeted him with a joke from a distance, Mrs Hattingh smiled, and only Carla stood motionless in the dimness of the doorway, unresponsive to the light or the excitement.

'Gerhard, you'll stay and eat with us won't you?' asked

Mrs Hattingh, bending to kiss him where he stood a step below her.

'Thanks, Aunt Mart, with pleasure.'

'Are your people alone in the house?' asked Mrs Hattingh.

'I told mother I might be a little late getting back. You know what she's like: she's not a nervous woman.'

'We'll eat immediately,' Mrs Hattingh promised, 'then you can still be home early. It gets dark quickly these days.'

'Mother has spent a night alone often enough, Aunt Mart.'

'Yes, of course.' Mrs Hattingh stood back to let him enter the kitchen. 'But you shouldn't drive around alone like this in the evenings, Gerhard, it's not safe.'

'Hello, Carla,' said Gerhard to the girl who was still leaning against the door-frame, and she put out a hand in greeting. The other man followed him inside and Mrs Hattingh called Carla to help her with the meal.

'Come, George, sit.' Hattingh slapped George's shoulder. 'You must be hungry. What were you up to this afternoon?' Hendrik and Johannes chatted with Gerhard, their voices low, the words inaudible, and the women were busy at the stove. Unnoticed, Paul also appeared and stood next to George. 'Look out for Gerhard,' he whispered. 'He's dangerous. He only came to find out who you are.' Then he moved away, taking a place on the other side of the table, before George could decide whether he had spoken jokingly or in earnest.

The women brought dishes of food to the table: there was baked pumpkin and beans, and a jug of water. 'If we'd known you were coming we'd have killed a sheep,' said Hattingh and everyone laughed.

For the first time, as he sat among them at table, George realized how much reserve and caution there had been in the apparent cordiality with which he had been welcomed here: he had been received as Uncle George Neethling's grandson, but a whole life, a whole world still separated him from those people. Now a visitor whom they fully trusted had come, and they spoke loudly and animatedly, and laughed heartily.

He ate and listened, taking no part in the conversation. From where he sat he looked at their faces in the glow of the setting sun, for the door still stood open and opposite him the last daylight slipped slowly across the wall, in gold, which became deeper and dimmer, until there was only a dull red flush, scarcely perceptible in the gathering dusk. Gerhard sat opposite him with Hattingh and Johannes on either side of him: they leaned forward discussing matters about which he knew nothing and laughing at jokes which he didn't understand. Mrs Hattingh handed out plates, urging them to eat more, and only Carla was quiet where she sat beside him.

'I'll make coffee,' said Mrs Hattingh and Carla got up to help her. Mrs Hattingh switched on the light: it was now quite dark.

'It's time I went,' said Gerhard.

'Just have a cup of coffee,' said Mrs Hattingh. 'You can surely stay for five minutes.'

'Five minutes, then.' The group at the table had already broken up, however. The women were once more busy at the sink and stove and the men were beginning to get to their feet. Only Gerhard remained seated, leaning over to George.

'And so, what do you think of the world around here?' The question was brisk and purposeful, not just an expression of courtesy, and his eyes again examined George's face keenly.

What could he say? Must all the confused and conflicting impressions be condensed in a single sentence under that interrogatory gaze? 'It's not what I expected it to be.'

'Do you people over there know nothing of our situation then?'

'We know in a general way how things are, but there's no direct contact, reports are vague, and one doesn't know what to believe.'

'Does it still matter to you?' His businesslike manner was unchanged, the question so cool and neutral that one could not suspect any bitterness behind it.

'Everyone still hopes to return, everyone waits for the day. My father worked with refugees, helped them with money or work or documents — whatever they needed. My mother was sick for home until the day of her death . . .' The electric light shone in his eyes, the dying glow of daylight no longer visible on the wall. She had longed, and in moments of confusion had called out names which he hadn't recognized but only with difficulty could he still remember the details, the movement of her head, her hand, her bracelet.

'And what are you doing about it?' Gerhard asked in the same measured tone.

'We use what influence we have, we exert pressure, we collect money . . .'

At the table, partly cleared, where Gerhard sat listening to him, the words, the activities themselves, sounded meaningless. And on whose behalf was he speaking? He meant his father, other people, for since his mother's death he had lost all contact with the world of the exiles. 'They wait,' he said. 'They wait to return.'

Gerhard laughed to himself. 'You people will never come back,' he said softly.

'Careful now, Gerhard, go slow,' said Hattingh, next to him, with a note of warning, but he paid no attention.

Hendrik and Johannes stood together, talking, at the other end of the kitchen. Paul had also got up; only the three of them remained sitting. What did this interrogation mean and why did Gerhard smile in patronising fashion?

'You people do nothing,' he said in the same soft, genial voice. 'You talk, you've spent hours, days, years already, talking, but it's we who remain behind who must do the work.'

Mrs Hattingh had made the coffee and came back now with the coffee-pot, but she stood at a distance from the table as if unwilling to interrupt their discussion.

'Coffee's here, Gerhard,' said Hattingh.

'I'll have to hurry with it so that I can go: it's dark already.'

Carla brought cups and Mrs Hattingh poured coffee; Johannes and Hendrik also came nearer and discussion became general. Was there a threat behind Gerhard's words, George wondered, a challenge perhaps, or rejection? Gerhard threw his head back, laughing at something Johannes said, and then he jumped up and began to say his farewells.

'But where's Carla disappeared to?' said Mrs Hattingh. 'Paul, go and look for Carla, tell her Gerhard's leaving.'

They had all risen to say goodbye to Gerhard but as he shook hands with George, he drew him aside.

'Why did you come here?' he asked.

George looked at him. He was handsome but behind

his good looks there was something more of which one only gradually became aware: those clear grey eyes could become cold and hard; his lips were thin, the jawline determined. Yes, he realized, Paul's warning had been seriously meant.

'I inherited Rietvlei from my mother . . .'

'I know that. I've heard it already. But what made you come out all the way?'

The answer to this question he had not yet clearly formulated for himself. 'Because it's a family farm, a farm I've inherited,' he said slowly. 'Because I knew it myself in the old days and grew up with stories about it. Because it still means something, I don't know what.'

Gerhard did not answer straightaway. 'We'll talk about it again,' he said.

'I'm leaving tomorrow.'

'You've been away a life-time, you can't run away after two days. We'll talk again.' Then he was gone and Mrs Hattingh and his sons followed him.

'He shouldn't be driving around so late,' said Mrs Hattingh.

'Is it so far?' George asked.

'Oh, Kommando Drift is just off the main road, but it's not safe alone after dark.' She began to collect the cups. 'He's not afraid of anything, he's still young . . .'

From outside he heard neither voices nor the starting of a motor to signal Gerhard's departure. 'Who are his people?' he asked, just for something to say.

'His parents came to the farm during the troubles; they were townspeople, like us. Kommando Drift is actually his mother's farm, Kotie's: she was Uncle Klasie's daughter. But where's Carla got to?' she said impatiently, breaking off her explanation. 'We hadn't even finished coffee when she was off without a word. What did Gerhard drive all the way for? And now Paul's disappeared after her. It's as if the earth swallows them up.' She went to the passage door, calling into the darkness. 'Carla! Paul!' There was no answer, and after a short while she sighed and came back to the table where George still sat. She looked around vaguely and then remembered what they'd been talking about. She came to sit opposite him. In the dim light she looked old and tired as she leaned forward, her arms on the table. 'It was Kotie's farm, Frank wasn't a farmer. He was too carefree for this sort of life and he never really fitted in here. Anyway, he got mixed up in all sorts of things, more out of mischief than for any other reason —so I've always thought— and then they came and took him away. Kotie sat at home, not even knowing where he was; it was days before she found out what had happened.' She looked at the oil-cloth on the table and then lifted up her head to listen, but there was no sound. The house was silent and they could hear no voices outside.

Where was Carla? Where was Paul? He saw the kitchen in the weak lamplight, the table, the woman opposite him, waiting and listening and then once more being reminded of a past grief about which she had been telling him. 'So Frank was taken away,' she resumed, 'and a few months later they came to tell her he was dead.'

'What happened to him?'

She made a dismissive gesture. 'People disappear, people die, and you never hear any more about it. A person's life is no longer important. You get used to it, and you learn not to ask any questions.'

Outside they heard a car engine running and Mrs Hattingh half turned on her chair to look at the passage-door. No-one came.

'So Frank never came back,' she continued, but her thoughts were obviously only partly on what she was saying, while she listened to the throb of the engine in the yard and the silence inside. 'Old Uncle Klasie died shortly afterwards and Kotie was left alone. Aunt Maria couldn't do much any longer and Gerhard was still a child. But Kotie managed the farm alone with only the old woman and the boy to help her: she ploughed and threshed and sheared the sheep and slaughtered like a man, and I never once heard her complain. It was as if all her troubles gave her new spirit.'

The truck turned in the yard: for an instant the headlamps flashed through the open kitchen door and then the sound of the motor died away in the night. Mrs Hattingh stared at the pattern of the oilcloth.

'It was good to see Gerhard again,' said Hattingh as he entered. 'We have you to thank for it, George. You're an important man in the district, you know. I hear that Bettie even wanted to drag you away to school this morning to show you to the children. I only hope we're not making you feel uncomfortable with all our attentions.'

'Where were you all the time, Paul?' asked Mrs Hattingh. 'And where's Carla?'

George hadn't seen Paul returning. 'She's in her room, Ma.'

'Couldn't she even come and say good-bye to Gerhard? What's the matter with her?'

'Surely you know by this time what's the matter with her,' said Paul as he came to sit next to George. Johannes and Hendrik hadn't come back and outside all was once again silent.

'Gerhard thinks it would be a good idea if everyone in the district had a chance to meet George,' said Hattingh. 'He's suggested that all of us come over to Kommando Drift tomorrow evening. What do you think, George?'

His wife looked up at once. 'That'll be Kotie's idea. That's why she didn't come with him this evening.'

'I should have left yesterday,' George said.

'But you let yourself be pursuaded to stay another day. What do you think: can we persuade you once again? Surely you can give us one more day?'

'I know Aunt Maria will be very glad to see you,' said Mrs Hattingh. 'She knew your grandparents very well.'

'He wants to ask the Lourenses of Eensgevonden, and of course Aunt Miemie and her lot from Moedersgift. It'll be a whole get-together: probably twenty, thirty people counting the children.'

'It means driving by night,' said Mrs Hattingh.

'We can get together with the Moedersgift people, it's less dangerous. If we leave here before dark, nothing can happen.'

'And we can always sleep over at Kommando Drift,' said his wife. Her eyes were bright and her face was flushed with excitement. 'It's ages since we were all together. When was the last time, I wonder?'

'You can put off going just for one day, can't you, George?' asked Hattingh. 'After that we won't try to keep you here longer if you want to go.'

'All right,' he said after a while. 'Just one day.'

'It's worth staying just to see Aunt Maria,' said Paul, laughing.

'Paul!' his mother exclaimed angrily.

'And Aunt Loekie Lourens is also someone you won't forget in a hurry. After you've seen that bunch together, you won't want to stay any longer,' he added softly while his parents began to talk about the arrangements which had to be made for the party. Johannes would have to drive to Moedersgift to let Aunt Miemie know, Gerhard to Eensgevonden; there'd be baking to do, too.

'I think I must go to bed,' George said standing up. 'I'm very tired this evening.'

'I'm sure it's tiring, this strange country and all the new people you're meeting,' said Hattingh.

'Didn't you sleep well last night?' asked Mrs Hattingh. 'Or was all the driving too much for you? It's a long way to Moedersgift.'

He shook off their concern and said goodnight. When he had closed the kitchen-door behind him, he stood quite blinded by the dark: there was no light in the passage, he remembered, feeling for the wall. He wondered if he would be able to find his room and was about to return to the kitchen when he saw the darkness lightening in the distance. Somewhere around a corner or from one of the rooms flickering light was coming nearer, flushing out the dark, growing clearer on walls and ceiling. It was Carla, a candle in hand, coming towards him from the far end of the long passage. She moved quickly, holding the candle high with the light falling on her face, and she was already close to him before she saw him and stood still.

Where she had been all this time and where had she come from, candle in hand? She said nothing and he felt he couldn't ask her.

'Goodnight,' he said, and walked past her to his room. In the candle-light he saw that she was looking thoughtfully at him and then she nodded slowly, almost formally. 'Goodnight,' she replied. She remained standing there, the candlestick held high to light him to his door, but as he was closing it behind him he saw that the passage was once again dark: she had blown out the candle or moved swiftly away with it.

'It's fine again today,' said Mrs Hattingh as she tipped the bread out of the tins. 'It's going to be a lovely day. You've had rather bad weather since you've been with us.' The aroma of fresh bread filled the kitchen. 'But you can see that autumn's coming. It's becoming chilly already — I felt it yesterday evening when Gerhard was leaving and the kitchen-door was open. And it's getting dark early. I must say I'm a bit nervous about going to Kommando Drift tonight.'

'Why is it dangerous by night?' asked George.

'We're so isolated here on the farm, anything can happen.'

'By day also, surely?'

'Not as easily as by night.' For a moment her attention was elsewhere, and he followed her gaze as she stared through the window, but there was nothing outside except the deserted yard in the pale early morning light.

'Help yourself to milk.' Mrs Hattingh pushed the milk-jug and sugar-bowl nearer. 'My husband and Hendrik left for town early this morning, as soon as they'd eaten. They had to take the potatoes to the Co-op.'

'Do you never go to town yourself?'

'Agh, why should I go to town? It's better for us to stay

away. And in any case so few of the people we knew are left.'

'What became of them?'

'They've gone or they're dead — so many things have changed these days, it's no longer the world we knew. So it's better simply to stay at home. In any case there's enough to do here.'

He was asking the wrong questions, he realized, intruding tactlessly and stupidly on terrain forbidden to him as an outsider.

'Did only the two of them go?' he asked, trying to change the direction of the conversation.

'Yes: two are enough. I must go and look for eggs,' she said suddenly and started fastening a scarf round her head. 'Take more coffee, if you feel like it: the coffee-pot's on the stove.'

Johannes came in through the back-door, greeting his mother and nodding at George, and sat down opposite him at the table. 'It seems to me that you people sleep late abroad,' he said with a gruff attempt at cordiality.

'I start work at nine or ten o'clock. I'm not used to getting up early.'

'You must lend a hand with the work here on the farm. You'll find enough to keep you busy from before dawn until late evening.'

'I don't think I'll try.'

'What's wrong with farm-work?'

'I don't mean there's anything wrong with it. But if I had to try to help you people, I'd be more of a hindrance than anything else.'

'Yes, that's true. You're a desk-man. Just look at your hands.'

George looked. On the day after his return he had an

appointment with the hairdresser and the manicurist would attend to his hands — only two more days in this foreign country of which he actually had seen very little and one more day on this farm with its huge kitchen, the silence outside, and Johannes in dirty khaki working-clothes.

Johannes was still looking at George's hands in a mocking but not unfriendly manner. 'If you decide to stay, we can always try and make a farmer out of you,' he said.

'Must I try to rebuild Rietvlei?'

'Why not? Many people have started with just as little, or even less. We'll teach you to lay bricks and sink a bore-hole, drive a tractor . . .'

'Do you think it's worth the effort?'

'Do you think so yourself?' Johannes asked in turn, leaning forward, his elbows on the table. Mrs Hattingh took a basket and went outside; they were alone in the kitchen. 'What are your plans for the farm?' he asked in a confidential manner.

'To sell it. That was always my intention and I haven't changed it.'

'Do you think you'll find a buyer?'

'I can try.' It wasn't any of Johannes's business, he thought; this new friendliness bordered on the intrusive.

Johannes laughed softly. 'You don't want to discuss it with me, do you? Don't you trust me?' It was clear that he was trying to be friendly, but in his mask-like face his eyes remained alert and searching. There was some covert reason for the interrogation, George realized, and felt that it was becoming oppressive. He got up.

'I'm sure you've a lot to do. I won't keep you.'

The words were intended to end the conversation, and

Johannes realized it but he went on smiling and seemed not to know how to react.

'What are you going to do?' he called after George.

'I'm going for a walk.'

'Where to?'

'I don't know; I don't care.'

Paul and Carla must be somewhere about the house, George thought as he left the kitchen and walked down the passage, and he wondered if he would be able to find one of them. On both sides of the passage there were closed doors; behind them the rooms were silent. When he stood still he heard no sound at all in the house.

Purposeless, he stared through a window at an empty yard, where nothing moved but the patterns of sun and shade. Beyond the fence and the blue-gums the veld lay waiting, but although he had told Johannes that he was going walking, he didn't feel like it. Rather he felt the need for someone to talk to, even if it was only Paul with his changing moods and unpredictability, or Carla who silently judged and censured him.

He wandered on through the house, through unused rooms with the same musty smell of decay which had oppressed him the day before at Moedersgift. Then he opened a door at the end of a passage and found himself at the top of some steps leading to a shed where he could hear something rustling in the straw. Someone was moving behind the bales of chaff which were piled up here, he realized, when his eyes became accustomed to the faint light, and he stood without saying anything, while the rustling continued, until Mrs Hattingh appeared from behind the bales, bent over with the basket in her hand. She didn't notice him and and went on scratching about in the straw, an old woman with wisps clinging to her

clothes, frowning a little and talking softly and plaintively
to herself. Watching her he felt a sudden pity: she looked
so old and shabby, searching here and there in the straw.
He approached her to offer help, but she gave a choking
cry and stretched out her hand to ward him off with such
terror on her face that he stood still in astonishment.

'It's me, Mrs Hattingh,' he said, and then she
recognized him.

'Oh, George, you gave me such a fright!'

'I didn't think I'd frighten you, Mrs Hattingh. I walked
through the house and came out here . . .'

'You mustn't scare me so,' she said with a certain
sharpness, as she bent to pick up the basket which she'd
dropped, and he saw that she was trembling.

'I'm sorry . . .'

'You don't know who could suddenly appear before
you. Hennie and the others aren't even at home . . .' She
was still trembling and he didn't know what he could say
to put things right.

'Can I help you?'

'What? Oh yes,' she remembered, 'the eggs — I
thought I'd better come and look for eggs here: a few of
the hens got out of the fowl-run and they've been laying
all over the place. I must look and see if I can find out
where they've nested. So far I've found nothing.'

She began scuffing again a bit aimlessly in the straw.
'Can I help?' he said again, but she seemed not to hear
him.

'The children must be here somewhere, but I don't
know where. They come and go as they please: one can't
keep track of them.'

'Shall I try and find them for you?'

'Oh, just leave them. They're young; let them get up to

what they like.' She bent to get under a cross-beam and stood in front of him. 'Hendrik and Johannes are quite different: they've a much stronger sense of duty; they're much more serious. But, of course, they're older...' He followed her as, still talking, she walked on. 'They came with us to the farm when they were small; the other two were born here — it makes a difference. And they're still so young — just children...'

Once more she had company, a listener to whom she could express her thoughts. Somewhat ill at ease George followed her, wondering how he was to get away again.

She stood in the door of the shed and looked out over the yard. 'The breeze is chilly,' she remarked. In spite of her prediction that morning, the day was not pleasant and the wind was cold. 'But all the same I don't think we'll get rain. If we have to battle through mud as well to get to Kommando Drift this evening... it's quite a distance even though they're our nearest neighbours.'

'The farms here lie far apart.'

'So many people have left, there are so many abandoned farms. It's just here and there that you still find people. But at least I don't have to be alone at home all day like Kotie: there's always somebody about, my husband or one of the children. Gerhard usually spends the whole day away in the fields, and Kotie can't leave Aunt Maria alone, so she just stays at home. The old woman isn't altogether helpless —she still does quite a bit in the house— and Kotie's a good shot, but I'd be afraid to be on my own like that.' Her attention was not on what she was saying and her words became incoherent: she was thinking about the eggs she had to look for and she was already tying her head-scarf tighter against the tugging gusts of wind.

'You also need the the temperament to be able to live on a farm,' he said. 'My mother always said that she could never have spent her life at Rietvlei.'

'Dear God, no. If you have a choice, it's another matter. With Kotie it was just the opposite, it was Frank who could never get on here, so she went away with him when they married, although she always remained a farm-person at heart. But most of us didn't even have a choice; it was a case of getting away and coming here or being trampled underfoot, those of us who couldn't leave in time.'

She spoke with some bitterness, but the remark was not directed at him. She had already moved away from him, searching among the drums and crates which stood against the wall of the store-room. 'No,' she said again, 'we had no choice. How should I have ended up on a farm otherwise? Of course sometimes we used to visit people on farms when I was young and then you could hear the mistress of the house ordering the servants about in the kitchen or her husband complaining about the labourers or the drought or the harvest, but that's all I ever knew about farm-life. How could I have imagined that I'd land up here, that I would end my life like this! Who could ever have thought that it would happen to us?'

She walked on, past the stone wall of the cattle-pen. 'I'm not a farm-person,' she said with vehemence. 'I didn't grow up like this, I knew a better way of life. Perhaps I should try to forget it, I don't know. Perhaps it's lucky for the children that they know only this sort of existence. I don't care about myself, I've had better things and, after all, my life's nearly over, but you want so much to give them something else, something that's worth all the effort.' She turned swiftly and looked at him almost apologetically. She had been talking to herself, forgetting entirely that he was there and listening; her words had not been meant for him.

'There don't seem to be nests anywhere here', he said.

'Oh yes — the eggs.' She knotted her headscarf tighter. 'Perhaps on the other side of the orchard: I've seen hens there. I'll go and look.'

Crossing the yard swiftly in the direction of the orchard, basket in hand, she left him. He stood looking after her and then he heard someone whistling behind him and saw Paul standing in the doorway of one of the outside rooms.

'I thought Ma would never let you go,' he called out, laughing. 'It's hard to get away once she's got hold of you.'

'Were you following us?'

'I heard you talking in the shed.'

'Where were you?'

'Hiding.'

'Why?' A conversation with Paul was always a matter of asking questions and eliciting answers one by one, for the boy seemed to enjoy giving information piecemeal.

'Why not? Why must everybody know where we are? Are you coming? We're going to read.'

'Who's "we"?'

'Me and Carla.'

'What about Johannes?'

'We're up in the loft — Johannes doesn't even know it exists: it's our place. Are you coming? Quickly, he might see us.' He was already running off and George followed him to the shed where, as on the first occasion, they climbed into the loft and pulled themselves up to the door, which Paul bolted behind them. Then, bending under the low roof, they reached the upper loft where Carla was sitting on the floor, waiting for them.

'We thought you'd probably prefer coming here to helping Ma look for eggs,' she said.

'I didn't know you two were here.'

'That's why we come here — so that no-one will know where we are.'

'Johannes knows,' said Carla.

'Johannes knows nothing: he just guesses.'

'And what's the difference to us whether he knows we're here or just guesses?'

'Don't sit and yap. We said we were going to read this morning. Pa and Hendrik will be back soon.'

'You know Pa will never be back before lunchtime: we've got the whole morning. Sit down,' she said to George. 'Just be careful you don't dirty your smart clothes.'

Her words were somewhat mocking but she was already opening the book she had on her lap. Paul stretched out on the floor and lay waiting.

'What's the book?' George asked.

'Oh just something Paul borrowed from Fanie Raubenheimer. He's got quite a collection.'

'It hardly ever happens that he'll lend any of them,' said Paul. 'He prefers us to go to Moedersgift, and then we read to each other. Or he reads his poems to us.'

'And we usually hear more of his poems than anything else,' said Carla.

'They're not so bad.'

'No worse than most of the books they've got at Moedersgift.'

Paul's face darkened with anger. 'We said we were going to read,' he repeated. 'If you don't start now, I'm going.'

'Sometimes when there's not much doing on the farm, Paul and I come here and read to each other,' Carla explained, and then she bent her head and began to read.

' "Drowsily the old farmhouse lay sheltering behind the kindly shadows of its trees in the heat of summer noon. The family had withdrawn, after lunch, to the cool of their rooms, and the farm labourers, who had been busy watering the orchard and vegetable-garden, had taken advantage of the opportunity to disappear silently, so that the yard lay deserted under the fierce rays of the midday sun. . ." '

She read in a low clear voice, holding the book in both hands on her lap. Paul lay stretched out on the floor, his chin resting on his hands, and George had gone to sit opposite them with his back against the wall. Outside, clouds still drifted in front of the sun; through the narrow, dusty panes of the window, light fell in alternating patterns on the floor, now bright, now dull. From time to time the panes rattled suddenly in their frames, or the corrugated iron of the roof clattered briefly; something scraped on the roof above his head, and Carla's voice was lost among these intermittent sounds: the book held no interest for him nor was she able to give form to a narrative which lacked it. Was this autumn, this dreary loss of colour? he wondered, and remembered one holiday in the Dordogne among golden vineyards and forests when his mother had looked at the poplars and said something about the willows and poplars at home, changing colour in autumn along the stream and around the dam near the house. He was then still a schoolboy —why was he not at school that autumn?— and had driven with his parents through the Dordogne.

In a little restaurant on the road they had drunk wine and eaten truffles, and his mother had said something about the autumns of her youth. Silently he had listened to her —he was still only a child and in any case he was never a companion in conversation for her: her words were never directed at him— and he had pictured to himself some sort of barbaric splendour, a wealth of smouldering gold, blazing trees massed together in the glory of their going. Then they had driven on: the sunlight was hazy, and the farmers were busy harvesting nuts. He had never imagined anything like this bleak loft, gusts of wind rattling the panes and clouds driven along above a dull, deserted land.

Growing sunshine fell on the chests, the floor, the books; it fell on Carla and made her hair gleam as she sat with bowed head and read on. It was the first time he had seen her without the hostility, the wariness, the deliberate aloofness with which she still constantly tried to ward him off: she was dreamy, lost in thought, opposite him in the delicate light.

She looked up, directly into his eyes, and for a short while there was silence.

'Are you two listening?' she asked.

'What do you mean?' Paul was indignant. 'What else do you think we're doing?'

'I think you're both asleep. You haven't heard a word I've been reading. Did you listen?' she asked George.

'You just don't feel like reading this morning,' Paul interposed before George could answer. 'That's what's wrong with you.'

'Then tell me what the book's about if you've been following so attentively.'

'It's about a farm, a clergyman . . .'

'You see! "About a farm and a clergyman" and for that
I've already struggled through twelve pages!'

It was clear that she felt no inclination to read and got
more enjoyment out of trying to make Paul angry; this
morning she was in a playful mood unfamiliar to George.

'Oh come on, Carla,' said Paul. 'Soon Fanie will want
the book back, you know how he is about his books, and
then nothing will come of all the reading.'

'And you think that'll be a loss?' she asked, leaning her
head back against the wall. 'Paul lies dreaming and you're
obviously uncomfortable in the corner, worrying about
getting your clothes dirty. . .'

'I can think about things other than my clothes.'

'Well, what did I read about?'

'About a girl on a farm and a clergyman who came on a
visit. . .'

She laughed, and then she bent her head again over the
book and read on slowly. It was true, George realized,
Paul wasn't listening either; the boy's eyes had become
dull and it was clear that his thoughts bore no relation to
what was going on around him. George himself heard
only Carla's low, measured voice and not the words she
read, the feebly-written story about unreal people. Again
he looked at her where she sat opposite him, at her faded
working-clothes, her strong, square hands and cropped
hair, and again she looked up and saw him staring at her:
it was just for a few seconds between two words without
there being any break in the sentence she was reading.
Had she taken offence? he wondered, but couldn't tell
anything from her bent head and the even pace of her
voice. Then he realized that in fact there was a change in
her manner of reading: a barely-perceptible emphasis on
certain words and phrases, an earnestness just out of

proportion to the text she read and a self-consciousness which had earlier been lacking. She was trying to provoke Paul, he thought with amusement when he noticed it, but Paul still lay gazing dreamily, unconscious of anything untoward. Carla turned over the page and read on; the story hovered on the edge of parody: the farmer's wife, her daughter and the clergyman played their parts jerkily, almost convulsively, their nobility and virtue caricatured while Carla sat and read with that slight exaggeration, that gentle irony. He enjoyed what she was doing and smiled; when she looked up again she smiled back and read on with an even greater solemnity. Paul still noticed nothing, and suddenly it became a game between the two of them.

' "She was a lovely young girl, in the springtime of life," ' read Carla, ' "and with her laughing red lips and dreamy blue eyes which could on occasion sparkle so provocatively, she had already led many young men a dance, without having lost her heart to any one of them." ' Carla lifted her head again and caught his look and they both burst out laughing.

Paul stared at them in astonishment, his attention dragged back by the interruption. 'What's the matter now with you two?'

'You should pay more attention,' said Carla. 'Didn't I say you weren't listening?'

He looked from her to George, but George was still laughing, seized by an inexplicable lightheartedness, and he remained bewildered and suspicious as he sought some explanation. Then the puzzlement and suspicion died away and his face became severe.

'Very well then,' he said, standing up, 'if you want to be silly, I'll leave you here. I'm not going to waste my

time with such stupidity.' But he couldn't quite keep up
his effort to be dignified. 'It's you: you've been trying to
be funny the whole morning,' he reproached Carla
vehemently. 'You're not interested in the book: you just
want to attract attention.' Carla remained unmoved.
'You imagine you're someone special because Gerhard
drives over from Kommando Drift to see you and you
think you can play the fool with everyone like you do
with him. And he didn't even come because of you: you
know that as well as I do. . .' Before Carla's indifferent
smile his voice died away; he scowled, and then he turned
and ran out. They heard him stumbling through the outer
attic and banging the door to the shed behind him.
George and Carla were alone.

'Do you want to hear more?' said Carla, gesturing to
the book in her hand.

'Of course,' he said without meaning it.

'Then you can read on yourself,' she said, and threw
the book towards him so that it fell on the floor in front of
him. 'I've had enough of it.'

'Why did you keep on reading then?'

'For Paul's sake.'

'And yet now you've made him angry.'

'That's not difficult. But one can't always let Paul have
his own way.' She turned her head away and looked at the
light growing and fading behind the dusty panes. 'In half
an hour he'll have forgotten that he was angry and he'll be
back.'

'Must we wait for him?'

'You can do as you please. I'm going to stay here for as
long as no-one misses me at the house.'

'Your mother was looking for you. . .'

'Oh, Ma. . .' Her tone was friendly but impatient. 'Ma

probably knows well enough where we are, but she won't let on. In some ways she's very obliging.'

'But not your father?'

'Are you really interested?'

'In your father?'

'In us.'

'Why shouldn't I be interested?'

'One should rather ask why you should be. We can't possibly interest you: we're backward, simple farm-folk with whom you're spending a few days because you didn't know what else to do — I'm right, aren't I?'

'I stayed here of my own free will,' he asserted.

'Really? Why?'

She waited for his answer, but he couldn't think of one. 'Because I didn't know what else to do,' he conceded, and they both laughed.

'Have you got a cigarette for me?' she asked.

'Do you smoke only when you're alone with me?'

'I smoke when I'm in the mood. And you've got foreign cigarettes, not our home-rolled stuff.'

He stood up and crossed the room to give her a cigarette and light it for her. 'So there's something to be said for me after all,' he remarked.

She smoked in silence for a while. 'You mustn't take too much notice of what I say,' she said then. 'I warned you earlier, yesterday morning at Rietvlei.'

'And I told you that I preferred rudeness to silence. I'd rather you insulted me than behaved as if I didn't exist.'

She shrugged. 'Ma and Pa took possession of you. There's so much they wanted to ask and tell you, or rather so many things they want to say and can say only to you. Why should I come looking for your company?'

'Perhaps we two have more to say to one another.'

'What makes you think so?'

'It's a possibility, nothing more. We're about the same age, we're the same generation, whatever differences there may be between us.'

She was silent for a long while, smoking and apparently thinking about what he'd said. 'The generation after the troubles, the new generation. . . Perhaps one gets used to the silence,' she said then. 'You long for someone to whom you can talk, you wait, you hope, but when you get the opportunity the words have somehow frozen and there's nothing left to say.'

'Is there really nothing, or do you just not want to talk any more?'

She sat thinking and then went on as if she hadn't even heard the question. 'No,' she said. 'It's not that the words don't flow freely: it's that you've simply outgrown them; you've learnt to turn words into acts and you just don't need to talk any more. You've become self-sufficient.' She smiled. 'It's the old people who want to sit and talk, my parents and Aunt Miemie, but words don't help.'

'What alternative do you have?'

'Just wait. Wait — you'll see.' She smiled.

'Paul accused you of trying to be funny this morning,' George said. 'Now you're busy playing the fool with me just like you did with him.'

'Do you think so?'

'I don't know what you're up to. Are you trying to get rid of me because I bore you, or does this little game amuse you?'

'You want me to talk to you and I'm trying to, in my way: it's the only way I know. If it doesn't suit you, there's nothing I can do about it. You're free to go: you know where the door is.'

'I don't want to go away; I really do want to talk to you.'

'And I want to know why.'

'Because you interest me — yes, really, even though you believe that you can't possibly be of interest to me.'

'Must I take that as a compliment?'

'I mean that you're quite different from the girls I've known: you live in a different world. . .'

She leaned towards him with sudden eagerness. 'Tell me about them, the girls that you know. Are you engaged? Have you got a girl?'

'No.'

'But you must know some girls. You've got women friends.'

'A few.'

'Tell me about them. How do they look? What sort of clothes do they wear? What do they talk about?'

'You're still trying to play the fool with me.'

'You don't want to tell me anything,' she said. 'You reproached us with not trusting you, but you trust us even less. As long as you've been here you haven't revealed anything about yourself. You've voiced a few generalities because you couldn't get out of it, but beyond that you've spoken only about your parents, never about yourself. You've been frightfully polite, you've appreciated everything we did for you, you've said please and thank you, you've pretended it all interested you, but you haven't let us get a glimpse of you yourself. You can't reproach us with anything.'

'My life's so different from yours. . .'

'I'm also a person. Or didn't that occur to you? There are lots of things I can understand or guess at or feel by intuition. After all, I also went to school, I've read and listened to others and heard about other things, even though I've lived my whole life on the farm and spend all day in the yard and vegetable-garden. Who are you to come and look down on me and say that I wouldn't understand?'

'I didn't mean to offend you.'

'No,' she said rapidly, 'I'm sorry, I know you didn't mean it. But you do look down on us, don't you, poverty-stricken farmers living here at the back of beyond with their sheep and their mealies, trying to survive. And we're not people, not like you and your friends, and you can't talk to us about them. We've become less than people.' He tried to speak but she gave him no chance. 'No, it doesn't matter, look down on us if you like. But if you're no longer regarded as a person, if you're no longer treated as a person, you yourself begin to forget that you are a person. You lose your pride and your dignity; the only thing that still matters is to survive: you crawl and twist and debase yourself at the word of command — oh, I've seen it in my own parents, and I'm afraid, I'm so afraid of degenerating like that, more than I fear old age, or illness or poverty. That, that's the worst thing they've done to us. It doesn't matter that we've been chased away to this place, nothing matters. What I'm afraid of is not being a person any more, of not being able to do anything, of not meaning anything.'

She spoke with a quite unfamiliar vehemence which astonished him; sitting next to her on the chest, he looked at her, and she seemed so young and vulnerable that his voice was gentle when he began to speak, as if he were talking to a child. 'I'd like to help you people,' he said. 'I'd like to do something for you, even if you don't believe what I say. But what is there that I can do?'

'There's nothing. You've made your choice, you've gone away and built up a new life and left us behind. All you can do is give a bit of comfort to Ma and others like her, the older folk with all their memories. But we don't remember anything of the past, for us there aren't dreams or illusions any longer.'

'And this attic then, where you come to hide?'

'Yes, the attic. . .' she said. 'The attic is Paul's place, these are Paul's books, it's he who wants to lie here and dream of other things, other worlds. . .'

'And you? Don't you ever dream?'

'It would be senseless.'

'Must I believe you?'

'Oh, I used to have all sorts of dreams, but that's in the past.' She spoke impatiently as if of a weakness long ago.

'And you're happy like this?'

'Don't I seem happy to you?'

'Are you content?'

'Why shouldn't I be happy and content, in spite of everything?' she said challengingly. 'But of course you wouldn't understand that either.'

'No,' he said, 'I don't understand. I understand nothing, I admit. You people are strange, your life is strange to me, even though I was born here.'

'You sound surprised.'

'I didn't expect this strangeness; this visit was a return as far as I was concerned, a home-coming. I grew up among people who spoke only about this country and could think about nothing else. I had to learn all about it as if there were no other countries in the world, and yet I can barely recognize it.'

'Dates of battles, all of which were won, names of people who were all heroes, fine words and noble gestures, long lists of heroic deeds, injustices which must never be forgotten. . . Was that what they spoke about to you?'

'Yes,' he said.

'I also know all those things: I was taught them by old Mr Malan at the little school at Moedersgift. He had a bald head with a scar running right across it, where a soldier once hit him with the butt of his rifle. "Look here, just look at me!" he used to shout when he began to talk about the injustices, as if that was the greatest injustice of them all.' She smiled a little. 'They wasted years of our lives with those things, with their patriotic songs and speeches and sacred covenants. There wasn't any sense in it: the land they taught me about was just as strange to me as it is to you. They should rather have taught us how to keep quiet, how to forget, how to be humble and patient, how to stick it out and to cling to life whatever happens — that's what one needs to be able to live in this country.'

'And what should they have taught me?'

'I don't know — French or German or geometry or whatever you need in your sort of life, not all the old useless things.'

'Perhaps you're right. I certainly can't make use of what I did learn.'

'You won't stay here,' she said, 'I knew it. My people have been discussing the possibility of your coming to live here, returning to the farm. But I never expected you to.'

'Your brother began talking about it, this morning in the kitchen.'

'Johannes? He too?'

'He didn't seem to have much confidence in my ability to adapt to farm-life.'

'You'd never make a farmer. You don't want to in the first place.'

'No, I don't. It's a life one reads about in books: for me it's not something in the real world.' He looked at the book she had thrown aside on the floor, and they both smiled.

'And yet it's a good life,' she said. 'In spite of everything it can be good. And it's a lovely country, even though it doesn't appeal to you.'

'I never said that.'

'Yet it's true, isn't it?'

'I don't know what I feel about it. Sometimes it frightens me, and sometimes it moves me.'

'It is a lovely country,' she repeated. 'It's autumn now, in a few months it will be winter. You can't imagine how beautiful winter is here: the veld is bleached white, the sky is remote and pale. Everything is hushed, everything is waiting to begin afresh.' She turned her head away and spoke dreamily to herself. 'But you won't be here to see it; you'll never experience it.'

Tomorrow morning he would leave this place; he had a reservation on tomorrow night's 'plane for Zürich where it was now spring and the trees were beginning to bud in the parks. He wondered what time they'd land at Zürich and when he would get to Geneva.

Carla stood up. 'I must go,' she said. 'I've still work to do.'

'Aren't you going to wait for Paul?'

'Paul's forgotten about us or else his tantrum's lasted longer than usual. It's not worth waiting.'

She was already walking away from him. 'Thanks for the reading,' he said. 'And thanks for your company.'

She remained standing at the door, her back towards

him. 'I said that there was nothing you could do for me, but you've listened to me — that's no small thing. There's no-one here I can talk to. But just forget everything I've said.'

She was once more her usual self, gauche and ill at ease about the words tossed at him over her shoulder. Then she left swiftly, her footsteps dying away.

He picked up the book from which she'd been reading. The page was dog-eared, and he straightened it, closed the book and put it away. For a while he sat there waiting, although he didn't know for what or whom, but nothing happened, no-one came. Only the light and shade shifted continuously over the empty floor.

Hattingh and Hendrik didn't return until midday and over lunch told the others how long they'd been kept waiting, their difficulties in connection with forms, the attempt to get some necessary rubber-stamp, and the endless series of delays. Mrs Hattingh, who with the passage of time had become more and more restless, was once again at ease. Paul came into the kitchen late and took his place at the table without greeting anyone or answering his mother when she asked him where he'd been, and Carla, too, took no part in the conversation. It was Johannes who asked his father and brother questions about whom they'd seen and about prices and weights. He was sitting there like a new boy at school, thought George, while the conversation eddied around him, and suddenly he longed for people to whom he could talk, people who inhabited the same world as he did. On the

day he arrived back he had an arrangement to dine with
Pierre and Ève. He had promised to bring the wine: there
was to be *fricassée de poulet à l'ancienne*, Ève had said.
He'd bring a Côtes du Rhône or a Graves, he thought,
and longed for the candle-lit table and the company of his
friends. Tonight there was to be the gathering at
Kommando Drift, and the day after tomorrow he
would be in Geneva. Should he take Ève flowers, he
wondered, or the honey-coloured Greek sweets she
loved?

'What did you do today, Paul?' asked Hattingh, but
the boy didn't answer.

'You said we had to bed out the onions, Pa,' Carla
replied.

'I was talking to Paul.'

'One can guess what Paul did all day,' said Johannes
scornfully. 'He doesn't have to say anything.'

'And what did you do?' Paul asked. 'Walk around
keeping an eye on us?'

'There was nothing to keep an eye on. You saw to it
that you disappeared the moment Pa's back was turned,
you and Carla both.'

'Did you go around looking for us?' asked Carla. 'I
didn't know you were so interested in what we did.'

'Children!' warned Mrs Hattingh.

'That's enough now,' said her husband. 'I don't know
why you always have to squabble among yourselves.'

'Paul still hasn't told us what he was doing all
morning,' said Hendrik, but no-one followed up his
remark.

'What time must we leave this evening?' Mrs Hattingh
asked her husband, and they began to discuss the
arrangements. It was decided that Johannes would fetch

Aunt Miemie and the others in the pick-up, while the rest of the family would drive with George. Paul and Carla took no part in the discussion, each busy with private thoughts.

'Do you think we'll have to iron your white dress before you wear it, Carla?' asked her mother.

'You know I don't like the white dress.'

'Whether you like it or not is another matter: it's the only one you have to wear.'

'What's wrong with what I'm wearing now?'

'If Gerhard likes her in her working-clothes, why do you trouble yourself about white dresses?' asked Johannes.

'It's a special occasion tonight: the whole district will be there and if you think I'm going to let you appear as you are, you're making a mistake.' Mrs Hattingh spoke quickly and excitedly. 'It's time you began to behave properly. What will people think about you?' Then she remembered George's presence and broke off suddenly. 'Go and fetch the white dress so that I can iron it.'

'You mustn't leave here too late, Johannes,' said Hattingh. 'You know what a time it takes for Aunt Miemie to get ready.'

The family got up, each one going his own way. Only Paul remained behind, playing with the bread-crumbs on the table.

'Are you still cross with us?' George asked, and the boy smiled as if he had been waiting for some such approach.

'I wasn't cross with you, only with Carla who is always trying to be funny.'

'You weren't even listening to what she was reading.'

'It doesn't matter to me about the book, it's only something Fanie gave me yesterday, something he didn't want himself.'

'Then why did you get so angry?'

'If she's going to play the fool with everything, there's no point in our going to hide in the attic: we might as well be planting out the onions. It's always been our special place, just for the two of us, but Carla's not interested in it any more.'

'You can keep it for yourself.'

'It's not worth the bother.'

'Paul, you must go and sit somewhere else,' said Mrs Hattingh coming from the pantry and beginning mechanically to roll up the sleeves of her cardigan. 'You're just in the way here.'

'Where are you going?' Paul asked as George stood up.

'To my room. I want to change.'

'There's lots of time before we leave.'

'I haven't got anything else to do.' The sky was still clouded over, but there was no more wind; he stood at the window and watched Johannes drive across the yard on his way to fetch Aunt Miemie. Behind him, Mrs Hattingh had put the flat-iron on the stove to get hot. Pierre and Ève would ask him about his visit, but what was there he could tell them?

'May I come with you?' Paul asked.

'Where?' he replied absentmindedly.

'To your room.' When George nodded and moved away, Paul followed gratefully. He was withdrawn that afternoon and in the room sat in silence on the bed watching while George, made somewhat uneasy by his interest, selected clothes.

'What are you going to wear?' When George showed him the suit, shirt and tie, he came over at once to look at them. 'What did that tie cost?' he asked, but before

George could answer he had already seen the other clothes in the wardrobe and suitcase. 'Why did you bring so much stuff with you?'

'To wear — why else?'

'You have fine clothes.' He was busy taking the shirts out of the cupboard where they hung, one by one. 'Everyone will be looking at you at Kommando Drift.'

'You can borrow one of my shirts to wear if you want to.'

'Do you mean that?'

'Of course. Otherwise I wouldn't have said it.'

Thoughtfully Paul examined the shirts again. 'The pale purple one,' he said. 'I'm going to put it on straightaway.'

He let his khaki shirt drop to the floor and rubbed his cheek against his shoulder and arm to feel the soft texture of the new shirt as he put it on. 'What is it?'

'Silk.'

'How does one fasten the sleeves?' George gave him a pair of cuff-links and helped him to fasten them. 'You've got all sorts of strange things,' Paul commented.

'There's nothing strange about cuff-links.'

'Perhaps not to you.' He looked at himself in the mirror and then began to move about the room, investigating George's things further.

'What's this?'

'After-shave lotion.'

'And this?'

'Talc powder.'

The bottles and tubes obviously fascinated him, and he examined them one by one until his curiosity began to irritate George.

'Do you want a tie to wear with the shirt?' he asked to distract Paul's attention.

Paul pondered the question and inspected the ties George held up for him, but then he shook his head. 'If I arrive wearing a tie, they'll just laugh at me.'

'Would it be better if I didn't wear a tie either?'

'Oh it doesn't matter what you do: after all, you're a foreigner.' He stretched his hand out to take the ties, however, and started examining them but at that moment there was a knock on the door and Hattingh came in, almost unrecognizable in the unexpected formality of a white shirt and dark suit.

'I've just come to see if you're ready yet, George,' he said. 'Go and change now, Paul, we'll be leaving soon.'

'I'll be ready in five minutes,' George said, and Paul left the room. Hattingh made a reassuring gesture. 'No, don't rush, I don't want to hurry you. But Johannes will probably be here soon with Aunt Miemie and the others, and we must try to get to Kommando Drift before it gets dark. I hope that Paul isn't a nuisance to you with all his tales — once he begins he can talk non-stop, just like his mother's family: smooth tongues and full of tricks, the whole lot of them.' He lingered while George began to change. The work on the farm had obviously been laid aside together with the faded khaki clothes, and he seemed a little ill at ease in the constriction of jacket and collar.

'You can probably see that I don't wear these clothes every day,' he said, laughing apologetically. 'I bought this suit before Johannes was born. But it's a good one: I'll probably be buried in it.' The cut of the suit was indeed old-fashioned George saw when Hattingh turned to go, and the jacket was taut across shoulders which had grown too broad for it.

The whole family had put on their best clothes he

discovered when he went outside to where they were standing waiting for Johannes and the people from Moedersgift. Hendrik, as unrecognizable as his father in an immaculate white shirt, with rolled-up sleeves, was apparently busy teasing Paul about his coloured shirt but they fell silent when they saw George.

'We can only hope that Johannes manages to get Aunt Miemie into the pick-up,' said Hattingh. 'If she insists on going to see for herself that every door and window is locked, we'll be waiting here until midnight.'

'Paul, did you remember about the dairy door?' said his mother.

'Ma, I've told you already that I've locked every door,' he said impatiently.

'You say lots of things, but whether you've done them, that's another matter,' said Hendrik.

'Carla, you must take a jersey,' Mrs Hattingh interposed swiftly before Paul could answer. 'You know how cool the evenings are already.'

'I don't feel the cold so easily, Ma,' Carla said.

She stood to one side, aloof from her family, under the blue-gum trees, and when she turned towards them George didn't recognize her for a second. The white dress she was wearing had obviously been home-made — by herself or her mother — according to what antiquated pattern, he wondered, copied from what photographs come upon by chance in a newspaper or magazine? No-one could make that dress with its long, full skirt look attractive, and it was clear that Carla wore it unwillingly, just as uncomfortable in it as her father in his outfit. It didn't suit her and the efforts to make it delicate and feminine with puff-sleeves and bows rendered it all the more unsuitable for her, with her sun-burnt arms and short hair. She knew that she looked foolish and her expression briefly acknowledged it, but then she lifted her head, challenging him to be amused or to pity her.

'You look very smart,' she said. 'It's just an ordinary gathering of farming folk we're going to.'

'I've apparently brought the wrong clothes with me. You've never yet approved of anything I've worn.'

'The clothes are nice: they're just not right for farm-life.'

'Here comes the pick-up,' said Hendrik and they all looked at a cloud of dust on the road, a long way off.

'You can see that Aunt Miemie's with them,' said Hattingh. 'That's why Johannes is driving so slowly. She's always terrified there'll be an accident.'

They waited for the truck which approached along the road in whirling dust. 'I suppose Aunt Miemie doesn't often leave the house,' said George to break the silence in which he and Carla stood together under the trees.

'Almost never. I'm sure it's in your honour that she's let herself be tempted out tonight.'

'She hasn't even realized who I am.'

'You're young Kosie Neethling, son of Uncle George and Aunt Lottie: she's grasped that.'

'And the fact that Kosie is dead?'

'She doesn't speak about death: she doesn't acknowledge its existence. As far as she's concerned all the people who've gone are still alive and it's for them she's come tonight, for Kosie and Uncle George and Aunt Lottie. It's a kind of tribute to the past.'

The pick-up truck came nearer and then turned carefully into the gateway. Under the canvas hood George saw faces, and Raubenheimer leant out waving; in front Aunt Miemie sat bolt upright between Johannes and

Bettie, a little straw hat with nodding flowers on her head. Mrs Hattingh had hastened to welcome her and ask if she would like to get out of the car, but Hattingh was in a hurry and his voice overrode the women's flow of words. 'Come on, people, we must go,' he said, and began shepherding his family to George's car.

Raubenheimer was still hanging half out of the pick-up. 'Hallo, George, old man,' he called out and one of his waving hands struck George as he passed. 'I knew we'd see each other again before you left.' His hair was plastered down against his skull, carefully combed on either side of a faultless parting. There was a white handkerchief in the top pocket of his jacket and he smelt of soap. Even his spectacles glinted more brightly, as if they'd been polished for the occasion.

'I can ride in the truck,' Carla said, but her mother, excited by the sudden activity and all the people in the yard, pushed her into the car. 'Come on, Carla,' she said. 'We must go. The pick-up's full enough.'

Hattingh and his wife, Carla and Hendrik, drove in the car with George, behind the truck which was now carefully making its way across the yard again to the road. As they followed, they could see Raubenheimer looking back, from time to time hidden by clouds of dust above which he regularly reappeared, smiling benignly upon them. His fellow-passengers remained indistinguishable behind him in the shadow of the hood.

'Did all the children come along?' asked Mrs Hattingh. 'How many of them are there these days?'

'I don't know, Ma. About six or seven.'

'So many? Who are they all? The Botes children, the Steenkamp girl. . .' She counted them up silently and tried to distinguish across the distance the people in the back of the truck. 'There are seven people in the truck,' she said. 'Who's the seventh then?'

'Paul's also driving with them, Ma,' said Hendrik. 'Now he and Fanie can talk to their hearts' content.'

'But where do you see Paul, Hendrik?'

'Fanie was hoping Carla would drive in the pick-up,' said Hendrik. 'Didn't Ma hear her asking if she might?' He was in a good mood, excited like the others.

'Good gracious! Is that the Pieterse boy?' asked Mrs Hattingh, still busy with the people in front. 'He's grown.'

'If I'd gone in the truck, Paul could've driven the car,' said Carla.

'And what does it matter?'

'He wanted to.'

'Paul's getting too smart with his borrowed shirt and his driving about in cars,' said Hendrik. 'Fanie's poems are no longer good enough for him.'

Mrs Hattingh went on talking, asking questions which no-one answered; her husband looked at the veld and now and then made an observation about something he'd seen, and Carla, sitting beside him, lost her aloofness and turned around to see what he was pointing out. George had to give all his attention to the pot-holes and bumps in the road, and to avoiding the dust thrown up by the truck lumbering along in front of them. The people sitting at the back of the truck were slung from side to side as, bumping and jolting, their vehicle progressed, and Fanie clung with both hands to the back-panel while he remained gazing back at the car across the distance separating them.

'I don't know how Aunt Miemie can stand this shaking-up,' said Mrs Hattingh.

'Aunt Miemie's as tough as they come,' said her husband.

'Aunt Miemie wouldn't have stayed away from Kommando Drift tonight, Ma, even is she'd had to walk every inch of the way,' said Hendrik.

The sun was setting and its last level rays were in George's eyes as it shone out between the clouds and the horizon. The broad sweep of the sky glowed with flame and gold, but the sudden darkness characteristic of the country was creeping near. Minute by minute the richness of the sunset was extinguished before them. It would soon be nightfall.

'Here we are,' said Hattingh, although George could see nothing. Then the road curved, revealing in the dip before them a large white house flanked by outbuildings and trees, on the level ground where dusk was deepening, its windows glinting in the remaining light. The little truck bounded faster, speeding to the safety of the yard.

The white wall was bright in the evening light; the windows and doors, however, remained closed and the only sound was the barking of dogs, apparently tied up somewhere at the back of the house. Then the door opened and the passengers of both car and truck began to get out to greet one another, to embrace, to kiss. Hattingh grasped George's arm and introduced him. 'Anna Neethling's son — Kotie Snyman.'

'I'm happy to meet you, George,' she said, and he saw a middle-aged woman with a calm face, something about her mouth and eyes showing that she was Gerhard's mother. Gerhard himself appeared next to her. 'It's good that you've come,' he said holding out a hand to George. He was clean-shaven and wore the white shirt and dark trousers which all the young men had on, as if it were a uniform.

The women had crowded around the truck from which Aunt Miemie was being carefully extricated, and Gerhard was welcoming the men. Forgotten beside his car, George looked at the small group of people: only the white shirts of the men were still clearly distinguishable in the twilight. Of Aunt Miemie only the hat with its little bobbing flowers could be seen among the people surrounding her, but her voice dominated the babble of salutations as she organized the next stage of the expedition. Johannes had to come and help her; someone must take charge of her sticks or hand her her cardigan; someone else must offer a hand, an arm, a shoulder and impatiently she called for Bettie.

George heard someone laughing next to him: Paul had come to stand on the other side of the car. 'You'll never be sorry that you stayed on for tonight's affair,' he said. 'Tonight you'll see a circus which you won't come across anywhere else in the world.'

'What do you mean?' George asked but at that moment Raubenheimer, who had been waving from some distance away, approached.

'Greetings, George!' he called joyfully. 'We must take care of him tonight, Paul, mustn't we, and not let other people monopolize him, so that we'll have a chance for a proper talk. How about it? What do you say?' Paul remained on the other side of the car, showing no interest, but Raubenheimer didn't wait for his reaction. 'I hear you're a publisher,' he said in a confidential tone to

George.

'Not exactly. I work for a publishing house.'

'It must be very interesting; you must see many books, get many opportunities to read and so forth. Perhaps you remember I told you yesterday I write a bit of poetry and that I could show you some of my work if you're interested? I thought that possibly tonight. . .' George could see a roll of papers in Fanie's inside pocket; his jacket bulged.

'I don't know if there'll be an opportunity,' he said, choosing his words with care.

'Oh, we can make an opportunity. Somewhere we'll find a quiet corner: the house is big enough. What do you say, Paul?'

'We must go inside,' said Paul.

Aunt Miemie had appeared out of the truck and, accompanying her, the slow careful procession crossed the yard in the direction of the house; Mrs Hattingh and Aunt Kotie supported her on either side and Bettie followed with cardigans, scarves and bags. Now the men should unfold a canopy over her, thought George watching the procession, and the solemnity of her entry would be complete.

'Come on,' said Paul to him, taking no further notice of the teacher.

'Now children, where are you?' called Raubenheimer, his tone suddenly sharp and peremptory. 'Come on, we're going inside. And remember what I've told you: don't make me say it again tonight!'

George had completely forgotten about the children who'd come with the others from Moedersgift and he noticed them now for the first time where they remained huddled together next to the truck. Shepherded by

Raubenheimer they attached themselves to the others who had already reached the steps, trainbearers and acolytes to the grown-ups they were following.

'Come,' Paul repeated, and George followed him. Gerhard had also stayed back to look for him. 'Come on,' he said. 'Tonight you're the guest of honour.' He stretched out his arm to include George in the procession and lead him into the house, and his mother looked around as she was crossing the threshold with Aunt Miemie. 'Come in, George,' she said. 'You're a very welcome guest.'

'Is everyone here now?' asked Gerhard, and then he closed the door behind them and locked and bolted it.

The company was led along a passage into a large double-room, the two parts of which were connected by an arch. One half was lit by paraffin-lamps and in the middle was a great table, laid for a meal, with chairs on either side, and the other room stretched away in darkness. There was no furniture other than the table and chairs. On the walls hung the usual portraits of politicians and heroes, arranged symmetrically next to one another. The only splash of colour in the bare white room was a flag at one end of it in what was obviously the place of honour; otherwise it was bright, and somewhat musty, as clean and empty as if no-one ever used it, indeed, as if it was not supposed to be used: an area set aside for the celebration of some lofty and inexpressible mystery.

Aunt Miemie was led to a chair, the acolytes around her to hand over and receive handbags and wraps and cushions and sticks. Then she leaned back, apparently exhausted by her exertions, for she no longer spoke: she pressed her handbag to her breast and only her jaws moved mechanically and soundlessly while her eyes raked the table, already impatiently, almost greedily, examining what there was on it.

'I thought Wet and Loekie would have been here ages ago,' said Aunt Kotie. 'Now it's nearly dark and they haven't come yet.'

'Kotie, you know what Wet's like and you know what Loekie's like,' said Hattingh. 'Do you imagine that both of them together could arrive anywhere on time?'

People laughed and conversation became general, but the voices sounded too loudly in the echoing room. The house was old with large, high-ceilinged rooms, and the little group of guests looked lost, and their conversation was selfconscious.

'Bettie, when are we going to eat?' Aunt Miemie asked.

'Any minute now: we're just waiting for Uncle Wet and Aunt Loekie.'

'For whom?'

'Uncle Wet and Aunt Loekie Lourens from Eensge-vonden.'

'If the stream's full, they'll never get through. Klaas Lotter's Coloured boy was once swept away there, him and the horse and cart.'

No-one paid any attention to the remark; they stood there waiting, like Aunt Miemie, to eat.

'It's wonderful that she can still travel such a distance to get here,' Gerhard said to George. 'Every time I see her she surprises me. That woman has undergone more than you could ever imagine.'

'She's a bit confused again tonight,' said Raubenheimer, and then they heard the noise of a vehicle outside and the dogs, chained or locked up somewhere, began to bark again.

'It's the Lourenses,' said Gerhard, going with his

mother to welcome the new arrivals. Aunt Miemie, left by herself, nodded imperiously to Raubenheimer, and George was left with the schoolchildren who were standing waiting near the door, the boys in bleached khaki and the girls in white frocks too short for them, a silent group, scoured clean, with six pairs of eyes which devoured him. 'Good evening,' said George, but their eyes darted away in alarm and they didn't answer him.

There was chatting and laughter in the passage and suddenly the room seemed full of animated people all busy exchanging greetings, questions, answers. Hattingh's loud laugh could be heard, and the excitement of the women, and Aunt Miemie, who was trying to make herself heard, calling vainly for Bettie. 'George,' Gerhard said, 'these are the Lourenses, the last of our neighbours you have to meet.'

'Many of the last shall be first,' said Lourens, shaking George's hand vigorously and laughing. 'That's what I always say, isn't it so, Gerhard? Many of the last shall be first.'

'The last of the herd also gets into the kraal, as they say,' added his wife, 'even if it's just before dark, with Wet driving the truck for all he's worth. Come girls, come and say good-evening to Uncle George's grandson.'

George saw a middle-aged man with a ragged moustache, a woman with rouged cheeks, and three adolescent girls holding themselves back, shy and giggling, and enveloped in the pleats, frills and bows of their unfashionable dresses.

Their mother presented them to him. 'This is Johanna, this is Hendrika and this is Daniella. Look, girls, there are the children from Moedersgift: go and say hallo to them. Heavens!' she said as the girls reluctantly moved off, 'we could hardly believe it when Gerhard came to tell us who had turned up in our part of the world. And how do things here seem to you?'

'Listen, George,' said Lourens before he could answer her, 'let me tell you.' When George waited for him to continue, however, he just sucked at the ends of his moustache, screwing his eyes up as if searching for inspiration.

'Come on, people, we're going to eat,' announced Aunt Kotie. 'George, you're to sit here next to me, then I can see that you get enough.'

'We've killed a sheep for you!' called Gerhard. Everyone was busy shifting chairs and seating themselves. Raubenheimer arranged the children at the end of the table, and Aunt Miemie, somewhat overwhelmed by the bustle and noise in which everyone seemed to have forgotten her, was still looking fruitlessly about her for Bettie.

'Goodness, but you've gone to a lot of trouble, Kotie,' said Mrs Hattingh.

'Tonight you'll eat mutton such as you've never tasted in your life,' said Hattingh to George.

'And Mother's made quince salad,' said Kotie.

'Just think of it — Aunt Maria's quince salad!'

'But where is Aunt Maria?' asked Mrs Hattingh.

'Here she comes!' called Hattingh, and everyone rose to welcome her.

The woman who entered was so obese that she could barely squeeze through the doorway, and she moved forward with difficulty. So excessive was her bulk that her arms projected helplessly from her sides and her legs seemed scarcely able to bear the great weight. On her vast trunk the head, with its blue eyes and hair tied in a little bun, seemed comic, an addition absentmindedly made with no regard to proportion.

Hattingh, Gerhard and Kotie went to meet her and accompany her to her place, and she lingered a moment behind Aunt Miemie's chair. 'Miemie,' she said plaintively and the voice emanating from her unwieldy body was surprisingly sweet and clear. 'Miemie, it's so long since we've seen one another.' Aunt Miemie, her attention divided between the food on the table and the still-continuing search for Bettie, looked at her without recognition. Then she said 'Maria,' but Aunt Maria's presence did not seem fully to have penetrated her consciousness, and while the other woman bent, with effort, to kiss her, her eyes still roamed around the room and her jaws continued chewing automatically.

'Mother,' said Kotie, 'this is Anna Neethling's son, George.'

Aunt Maria halted on the way to her place to look at him. 'One can see whose son you are,' she said. 'One can see whose family you belong to.' Her hand was astonishingly tiny, delicate and soft in his: like the musical voice and the face with the alert eyes, it seemed to have no obvious connection with her body. 'You have your grandfather's name, and your grandfather's eyes. They all had lovely blue eyes like yours.'

Her words made him uneasy, as if the past for which he had searched in vain for days had suddenly been recalled, as if the wind had flung open doors and windows to drive a sudden chill before it through the room and make the lamps flicker.

Aunt Maria made her laborious way alongside the table to her chair, and when she had sunk into it the others approached one by one to greet her. Meanwhile Aunt

Kotie busied herself with plates and dishes.

'I'd better come and sit next to you straightaway,' Aunt Loekie said to George, 'before someone takes this place. Tell me, how are things with all of you over there?'

'Uncle Hennie, come and sit down,' Gerhard said, waiting behind his own chair. 'But where's Carla?' She had come in unnoticed with Aunt Maria and taken her place among the children and the Lourens girls at the other end of the table, and while Gerhard was still looking for Carla, Bettie seized the chair next to his.

'It's a long time since we were all under one roof,' Aunt Loekie said. 'And it's a long time since I tasted mutton, what do you say, Kotie? It's all due to your coming such a long way from overseas, George.'

'George, here's your plate,' said Aunt Kotie. 'Help yourself to salad: don't be shy.'

'Come, I'll help you,' Aunt Loekie offered. As she leaned across him to help him to food, he smelled her sickly perfume. Of all the women here, alike in their sober, old-fashioned clothes, she was the only one who had tried to look festive, with artificial flowers pinned to her shoulder, perfume and make-up. She was perhaps forty, not much more, but her rouge and eyebrow-pencil had been injudiciously applied and their hard lines made her face look hard too. Cheerfully she chattered on, barely giving him a chance to answer, while her husband sat listening, smiling benignly, at the other side of the table where he'd ended up next to Aunt Miemie.

'Come, George, give me your glass so that I can pour you a drink,' said Hattingh.

Gerhard knocked on the table. 'May we have quiet for a minute?' They all bowed their heads while he quickly and almost inaudibly said a prayer. Then the room was once more full of a confusion of talk, laughter, and the clatter of plates and cutlery.

'Your health, George,' called Hattingh, giving him a full glass. He took a mouthful and choked; tears came into his eyes and the people around him laughed and thumped him on the back. 'You've never tasted brandy like that overseas, have you?' said Hattingh. 'It's a speciality hereabouts, distilled according to our own recipe. It doesn't look anything wonderful but it's got the kick of a young horse.'

Everyone had begun eating: Mrs Hattingh had cut Aunt Miemie's food into tiny pieces, and the old woman crouched low over her plate, eating greedily and hurriedly with the same movement of the jaws as before; she took no notice of anyone. Sitting next to Gerhard, Bettie laughed shrilly.

'But, Mart, don't tell me that that's all you're going to eat tonight,' exhorted Kotie.

'I'll get some more, Kotie, thanks. I've more than enough.'

George looked up from his plate and saw Aunt Maria opposite him, huge behind the table, her food untouched while she looked at him, tranquil and pensive, and not at all put out when his gaze caught hers. She smiled slowly and nodded to him, a gesture of recognition and welcome, and he raised his glass and tried again to drink the mud-coloured liquid.

He heard Hattingh's voice. 'But it's after all not anything a person need be ashamed of. Gerhard feels that everything here tonight is probably very simple to you after what you're used to,' he explained to George. Drink had made him cheerful and his face was red.

'I didn't say I was ashamed, Uncle Hennie,' Gerhard

said calmly. 'I know nothing I should be ashamed of.'

'Of course not,' said George and Gerhard leaned forward to observe him more closely.

'Goodness, we can all guess what sort of fashionable life George is used to,' interposed Aunt Loekie.

'You know that's not how I meant it, Gerhard,' said Hattingh. 'But things have changed here, they've changed a great deal, and I only want George to understand that.'

'He'll understand it well enough. After all his mother was a Neethling of Rietvlei,' said Gerhard.

'You know yourself things would have been different in your late grandfather's time, and in George's grandfather's also. Yes, you young people get impatient when we begin talking about how it used to be, but I feel I must make it clear, for George's sake.'

Aunt Kotie, silent but alert at the head of the table, had taken George's plate to replenish it. 'Does our food taste good to you, George?' She had no doubt about his answer; calm and self-assured she sat at table, looking about her while her guests chatted and ate.

'It's not that we don't want to listen, Uncle Hennie,' said Gerhard. 'You know that yourself. As one gets older, the past begins to be more and more important and you want all the more to think about it, talk about it — it's easy to understand that. But when you're young you don't want to talk — you want to act, and then perhaps you seem impatient and intolerant.'

'No, no, man. Don't think that you've made me feel bad: I understand only too well how you young people feel. I've been young myself and impulsive, like you are, and I also have young sons. I sympathize with you people, you know that.'

'Some more salad, Aunt Miemie?' said Kotie softly so as not to interrupt the menfolk. Aunt Miemie was still bent over her plate, gravy running down her chin, and Mrs Hattingh came to help her with a table-napkin.

'My word, Aunt Maria, but you make the most wonderful salad,' called Aunt Loekie across the table and for a moment women's voice drowned the men's.

'But you young people are sometimes too impatient,' George heard Hattingh's voice, slightly slurred now, for drinks had been poured again. 'You'll forgive my saying so, but you tend to forget how important the past is, especially when one is working for the future.'

'That's something Uncle Hennie can't say about us, not about the young people here tonight.'

'George, why are you drinking so slowly?' asked Aunt Loekie.

'It's a powerful drink if one's not used to it.'

She laughed sharply. 'But when you've swallowed it, it makes you feel good. You must give it a try: you seem to me to be much too serious. Don't you think so, Kotie?'

'I think George enjoys everything in his own way. He just has to get used to us.'

At the other end of the table, where the young people were still noisy — Raubenheimer, Bettie, Paul, the Lourens girls and Carla — everyone now burst out laughing. One of the Lourens girls jumped up, her face purple, and fell giggling back into the arms of the people on either side of her.

'The young people are enjoying themselves,' said Aunt Loekie, a bit enviously.

'Carla is also very cheerful tonight,' said Aunt Kotie. 'These days she seems to me always so withdrawn, Mart.'

'It's a difficult age: she and Paul are both very moody.

What do you think, Aunt Maria?'

'But I'm telling you that you may not forget the past for a single moment,' declared Hattingh, and he slapped the table with his hand to emphasize his words, so that the women turned around in alarm. He wasn't angry: he pushed his plate away and sat back calmly talking to Gerhard. 'I'm saying it to you as an old man who has experienced a great deal, and felt much of it on my own flesh — when we die, we older folk, then those of you who remain behind mustn't forget what happened in our time; it must be as vivid to you as it is to us. There is no-one here of your mother's generation or your grand-mother's who doesn't bear scars.'

'Yes, God knows there's been enough shooting and murder and rape among those of us sitting here tonight,' observed Aunt Loekie thoughtfully, and she drank, her little finger extended.

'Loekie!' Mrs Hattingh's voice was reproachful and a little shocked, and Loekie took another gulp of her drink as if she had said nothing at all.

'Of course you must be idealistic,' Hattingh went on, 'it's right to want to struggle and fight, but a person must be clear about what he's fighting for, he must have the past as a foundation on which he can build.'

'Fight, yes, that's right, Uncle Hennie!' Lourens called. Sitting on the other side of the table he had heard the last remark. 'Now that's the sort of talk Gerhard likes to hear. What do you people think — are we going to fight a bit?'

'Whoa, Uncle Wet, let's finish eating and clear the table first,' said Johannes sitting next to him, smiling.

'Well, what about it: are we going to fight?' Lourens repeated with excitement. 'Just put a loaded gun in my hand — what do you say, Hennie?'

'There's not much chance, Wet, no-one feels like it. It seems to me that we of the old guard are more enterprising than the young lot.'

Lourens called out: 'I carry my gun in my good right hand and I dance with the girl from another land! How do you like that?' Until now he had been sitting quietly between Aunt Miemie and Johannes, but now that his reserve had broken, he couldn't be silenced: excitedly he whisked around on his chair, his eyes flashing. 'How's that? How's that?'

Aunt Loekie improved on it: 'I dance with the lad from another land! What do you say, George?'

'Yippee!' shouted her husband.

People sitting around him smiled, or were perhaps laughing at him. There was a smile on Gerhard's face too but his eyes were expressionless.

Bettie had once more turned her attention to their end of the table. 'What's Uncle Wet saying? Are we going to dance?'

The words passed from person to person along the table where the young people were sitting. 'Danie, Fanie's asking you for a waltz,' one of the Lourens girls said to her sister, and they collapsed again, breathless with laughter.

'They're a happy bunch of girls, those daughters of yours, Loekie,' Mrs Hattingh said. 'It's a long time since I heard anyone enjoy themselves so much.'

'And it's a long time since there's been so much laughter in this house,' Kotie said; she was putting covers back on dishes, and her face revealed nothing of what lay behind her words.

'There's been a lot of laughter in this room,' Aunt

Maria objected. 'And dancing and singing and music-making right through the night...'

'And much weeping and mourning also,' said Kotie briskly, still busy with the dishes, but her mother apparently didn't hear her.

'Do you still remember, Miemie?' Aunt Maria asked.

Aunt Miemie had scraped her plate clean with knife and fork and mopped up the last drops of gravy with a piece of bread. Now she had finished eating and she leaned back with hands folded, busy trying to make out where she was and what was happening around her.

Mrs Hattingh wiped Aunt Miemie's mouth for her. 'Aunt Miemie, Aunt Maria is talking to you,' she said loudly.

'What's the matter, Maria?' Aunt Miemie asked, blinking her eyes.

'Do you still remember the parties here at Kommando Drift in the old days?'

'I don't know why you didn't leave the red carpet down,' Aunt Miemie said with a dissatisfied air. 'I don't like the way you've furnished the house these days. Is this Kotie's taste?'

'Good heavens, Miemie, that carpet would have been more than forty years old if we still had it.'

'It's probably the way young people nowadays like things,' Aunt Miemie continued. 'But this room was pretty enough for me the way it was. And what did you do with the flowers? Don't tell me you've already thrown them all away?'

'What flowers are you talking about, Aunt Miemie?' asked Hattingh, who was listening to her out of politeness.

'All those flowers that were here, a whole truck full of them that Lottie brought over from Rietvlei.'

'That's the time the Minister was here,' said Kotie.

'Of course, yes, I remember,' said Hattingh. 'I was a mere child but that day all of us came along to Kommando Drift.'

'I've never baked so many milk-tarts in my life as I did that week,' Aunt Maria said reminiscently, a light smile passing over her face at the recollection.

'Tarts and cakes, a whole table full of them against the wall in this very room,' said Hattingh. 'Of course, we children weren't allowed in here — we had to play outside — but Kosie Neethling and I came in when no-one was looking and hid under the table, behind the table-cloth. Wet, do you still remember?'

'My goodness but that was a happy day!' Aunt Miemie had gradually begun to take part in the conversation again. 'How's it that you don't entertain like that any more, Maria? I must say that Kotie's way of doing things now doesn't appeal to me.'

'How could we possibly entertain like that now? Do you know how many sheep we killed for the barbecue that evening? And how many basketfuls of quinces I grated with my own hands for the salad?'

'What did the Minister come for?' asked Aunt Loekie.

'I don't remember exactly: he was probably Father's friend. How was it again, Ma? He came to hunt with Pa...'

'The whole district was here in this house that day,' said Hattingh. 'The Mayor and the whole Town Council.'

'Those bowls of jelly!' Lourens recalled. 'Green and red and yellow. And the puddings with nuts in them and the cherries and cream — a whole table of them! Everything a child's heart could want.'

'Please, Uncle Wet; I swear you're making me hungry

again,' Bettie called out, giggling, but the older people, all of them busy with memories, didn't hear her. Gerhard leaned forward to listen to them, his chin propped on his hand, smiling again with his mouth but not his eyes. Johannes, too, sat and listened, out of politeness rather than interest.

Lourens continued recalling the food. 'And there were ginger biscuits and soetkoekies.'

'Maria, when did I last taste your soetkoekies?' Aunt Miemie spoke accusingly. 'Why don't you bake them any more?'

'But Miemie, when did you last see a bottle of wine? How can I bake them if I haven't got sweet wine?'

'Help yourself to another drink, George,' said Aunt Loekie. 'You don't have to be so shy, does he Kotie?'

'You must make yourself quite at home here with us,' Aunt Kotie said. 'After all you're at home again aren't you — or not?' There was no sign of doubt in her grey eyes as she looked at him: it was a statement, not a question.

Unasked, Aunt Loekie poured him another drink and then filled her own glass again. She had become noticeably cheerful and George found that the alcohol was beginning to affect him too, so that the voices around him ebbed and flowed like swells on which he floated, volitionless.

'You came over from Moedersgift early that morning to help,' said Aunt Maria to Miemie. 'Lottie Neethling drove over from Rietvlei with the flowers and you came with her. Every maid on the farm had to jump to it in the kitchen!'

Unexpectedly Aunt Miemie spoke again. 'I wore my blue dress, with pearls,' she said. 'And the white hat with the veil and the pink roses.'

George looked at her sitting across the table from him, her jaws working, her hair fuzzy, and it seemed to him so improbable that he wondered if he had misheard her, but she had stated a fact, and she nodded with the completest satisfaction at the recollection of her glory.

'After dinner, the grown-ups danced,' said Aunt Kotie. 'I remember I was allowed to stay up to watch. This room was full of flowers.'

At the other end of the table there was still laughter and noise from the young people. One of the Lourens girls jumped up and fled shrieking, but when no-one followed her she returned her place. Raubenheimer was trying to perform a trick with knives, spoons and glasses: a glass of water fell over, and from everyone came a hubbub of laughing, screaming, calling out. Even the schoolchildren began to laugh among themselves.

'After dinner Okkie de Vos started telling jokes,' said Hattingh. 'Kotie, do you still remember him?'

'Yes, of course. And Aunt Joey with her paper-doilies. Such affectation!'

'They had that mob of impossible children,' Lourens declared.

'Now you're thinking of the Conradies. Uncle Okkie had only two daughters who never had a word to say for themselves.'

'But they were very pretty girls, those.'

'And one of them ran away with a Portuguese or did something odd.'

'Who? Who are you talking about?' Aunt Miemie asked eagerly.

'And there was Naas Moolman,' Kotie remembered.

'Naas and young Kosie Neethling were always up to

tricks. Kotie, do you still remember all those times we went over to Rietvlei in the old days to swim? And afterwards we had a barbecue and danced on the stoep.'

'We were always giving barbecue parties, too,' said Aunt Loekie to George, bored with other people's conversations. 'I was a town girl you know: my father was an auctioneer. We had a huge house and the young people always gathered there and we used to have music and dancing till all hours.'

'Oh yes, the Neethling children, Anna and Kosie. Whatever happened in the district was always started by those two.'

'Lord, but you youngsters were a godless lot.' Aunt Maria smiled as she spoke. George nodded at Aunt Loekie but tried to hear, above the sound of her voice, what the others were saying.

'Kotie, do you remember the time you and Kosie sat together on the swing and the rope broke?' Lourens called out excitedly.

'He was full of tricks,' said Aunt Kotie, shaking her head at the memory of something that had happened ages ago.

'And Anna . . .' said Hattingh.

'Anna Neethling was such a cute child, I always thought,' said Aunt Miemie. 'A bit unruly but as you get older you grow out of your wildness. She went overseas, didn't she? It's a long time since I've seen her.' The bracelet, thought George, the phials of medicine, the roses; the black veil which hid her face in the back of the chief mourner's car. You grow out of your wildness.

Aunt Loekie, nothing daunted, went on. 'The Mayor's son and the attorney's daughters . . .'

From the other side of the table, Mrs Hattingh joined

in. She was as out of it as Aunt Loekie, sitting among people who were recollecting things in which she'd played no part herself. 'Yes, and when I think of the time when I was still a girl... My mother always loved entertaining: hordes of people came to us because of my father's position...'

Aunt Loekie was already interrupting her but George couldn't hear what she was saying, for Hattingh had called across the table to him. 'George, it's your people we're talking about now.'

'Anna with her lovely blue eyes,' said Aunt Maria in a plaintive, musical voice. 'They all had such beautiful blue eyes. Do you remember, Miemie?'

Hattingh sighed. 'Those old days at Rietvlei,' he said. 'Those moonlight nights with the scent of Aunt Lottie's roses...'

'It wasn't hard to get lost in that garden,' Lourens declared, and winked at George.

'What'd a girl like that want to go overseas for now?' asked Aunt Miemie. 'But of course she always had grand ideas. What her father had to spend on her clothes, even then!'

'She always dressed so beautifully,' Aunt Kotie said.

'She was a lovely girl,' said Aunt Maria.

'In spite of everything,' added Aunt Miemie, reflectively. For a moment they were silent.

Mrs Hattingh was still reminiscing on the other side of the table. 'And when I was at University, my friends always came to us to swim at weekends. I was at University with Ben Meyer, you know...'

Aunt Loekie was barely listening. 'The magistrate and his wife were old friends of my parents,' she said. 'In the summer we used to rent a house together at the seaside . . .' They leaned towards each other over the table, but didn't even try to pretend that they were listening to one another; they simply sat and spoke with voices growing ever more urgent as they recapitulated the facts —the amounts, the servants, the guest-lists, the holiday resorts, friends, hotels, meals, clothes and cars — piling them up, layer upon layer, with almost desperate energy, as if they were busy building barricades of words and memories against the menace of reality.

'Oh,' cried Mrs Hattingh, 'that was a wonderful time! I didn't grow up like this.' She looked at the table with the remains of the meat and salad, at the room, bare in the lamplight, at the girls laughing and giggling together in their unfashionable, fluttering skirts.

'Nor did I,' said Aunt Loekie, 'I was used to better things.'

In the sudden silence at their end of the table her words were louder than she had intended.

'We were all used to better things, Loekie,' said Aunt Kotie crisply. 'Not one of us grew up in the way we have to bring up our children now.'

Aunt Loekie apparently didn't hear her. She stared before her, her glass clenched in her hand and her face contorted. 'Why couldn't it stay like that? Why did we have to lose it all?' She spoke in the passionate, reproachful tone of a child and for a moment no-one knew what to say. Interrupted in the middle of their conversation, their thoughts, their recollections, they looked at her half-uncomprehendingly, helpless in the face of this unexpected display of emotion.

'What more could we have wanted? We had everything. What did we do wrong, what did we do to deserve this? Why did we have to be punished like this? Do you call this a life?'

Were they embarrassed by her lack of self-control, or moved by her appeal? Was their silence a sign of agreement or disapproval? No-one spoke.

Then George saw that Gerhard had got to his feet. 'Friends,' he said, and banged on the table to attract their attention. The chatter and laughter of the young people gradually died away, and the older people turned towards him. 'Friends, we have come here to be sociable together, but I hope you'll forgive me if I say a few words before we go any further.'

'Good for you, Gerhard!' called Lourens and there was laughter and exclamation from the other end of the table.

'You know yourselves how seldom it is that we, who have remained in the district, get together. There's no need to try to make excuses for that, for you also know how difficult it has been made for us to keep in touch with one another. But such contact is important, because we few have a solemn, I would even say, a sacred task: we must defend our heritage against all the dangers which threaten it, and we must stand shoulder to shoulder to encourage and to support one another.'

Again they called out their assent. Bettie, who was sitting next to Gerhard, looked up at his face and clapped enthusiastically and Aunt Loekie also began to clap. In Aunt Kotie's eyes George saw the pride with which she listened to her son and, indeed, he spoke fluently and self-confidently, as if he were used to making speeches.

'For this reason it's always an exceptional occasion when we can come together as we have tonight,' he went on. 'But this evening there is another reason, a special reason, for our meeting. As you've probably already guessed, I mean the presence here of a grandson of Uncle

George and Aunt Lottie Neethling of Rietvlei, whom most of us can still remember well.'

They clapped and called out and turned around to look at George: he saw Bettie's face, shiny with the heat and the excitement; Raubenheimer who waved at him; Mrs Hattingh who nodded approvingly. Then Gerhard was speaking again.

'We are a small group who have remained behind here, robbed of all we possessed, surrounded and threatened by many enemies, and the only thing which gives us the courage to hold out is our inextinguishable faith in the justice of our cause. Sometimes, however, we get some slight encouragement, some sign or other that our struggle is not hopeless and to me George's visit is such a sign. After all the years of isolation, we are once again in touch with one of our own people from abroad and we realize that we have not been altogether forgotten: the fact that someone has even now returned shows that the ties of blood are stronger than all the artificial separation forced upon us. George, who went away from here as a child and grew up abroad as an exile, could not forget his past. Our country did not lose its hold over him: he came back to see the family farm once more and to pay homage to the memory of his forefathers. We are glad that he is here, we are glad to have him with us, but we hope that he will not content himself with a mere visit. May he show his love for the farm and the country, his respect for his ancestors, their trials and their struggles, and his feeling of being at one with his people, may he show all this in deeds as well!'

Gerhard's mouth was dry but his eyes sparkled and he spoke as one inspired. All those present sat looking at him, motionless, and even the children were quiet. Only

Aunt Miemie began to fidget, her eyes restlessly searching among the dishes and plates for scraps. Then she stretched out her hand to grope furtively among the dishes, and George, uneasy at Gerhard's words, followed her movements from where he sat, opposite her.

'That decision, however, we shall leave to him. Whatever consequences his visit here amongst us may have, I want to say just this on behalf of us all: George, you are welcome among us and we are happy to have you here.'

Aunt Miemie's hand moved more rapidly along the table to find something before Gerhard should finish speaking and attention might once more be directed at her. It was, however, already too late, for Gerhard made a gesture in George's direction and everyone began to applaud. He would have to reply, thought George, and stood up still searching for something to say.

'Ladies and gentlemen,' he said when everyone was quiet, and knew as he was saying it that his opening words struck a wrong note in that place and on that occasion, but it was already too late: they had been uttered. 'I want to thank you very much for the way in which you have made me welcome here. I came to visit Rietvlei, the farm on which my mother was born and grew up and which she never forgot . . .' Gerhard's eyes were fixed on him. No, he realized, it wouldn't do: he couldn't talk about his mother in that company, for the Anna Neethling he knew was not the Anna Neethling they remembered; how could he say anything about falling leaves in the forests and the nut harvest, roses, fashion-magazines, and tea-cups of the finest porcelain; how talk to them now about the woman with a pearl necklace, going into dinner on the arm of a former colonel, taking her place at table while she told him about the farm of her youth; how tell them about the woman in the chief mourners' car? They wouldn't understand.

'I myself scarcely still remember Rietvlei for I was a small child when we last visited the farm, but I always wanted to come back and see it. Now, at last, I have done so. . .' The rubble, the wild roses and shrubs — yes, these had been the goal of his journey, he thought, and yesterday he should have left. He saw Carla looking at him. Only Aunt Miemie wasn't listening, again busy with her search for what the table-top might hold. 'Not much, I discovered, remains of the farm, and my mother's family has died out. But all the same, I shall have pleasant recollections of this visit,' he added and thought he could see already the possible decorative turn of thought and phrase which he needed to conclude his short address, 'for I shall always remember the friendship you have shown to me and your hospitality. For everything, I thank you warmly.' He sat down and they clapped again, vigorously, enthusiastically, moved by the heat and the drink and the gathering, by his presence among them and their remembrance of his family, by the fluency and the ease with which he had expressed himself. Aunt Miemie alone was unmoved: she was intent on brushing bread-crumbs together with her finger.

All the womenfolk helped to clear the table and take the dishes and plates to the kitchen. The men drew together at one end of the room, rolled cigarettes, and talked.

'Just be patient a while, George, then we'll have some

music,' said Lourens. He rubbed his hands with pleasure at the prospect and joined a group of men standing and discussing winter fodder.

George walked idly through the room, looking at the portraits on the wall. The women were busy; the men had forgotten about him. Only the school-children watched his movements from where they had withdrawn into a corner. The gaze of those alert eyes in the narrow, indecipherable young faces made him feel uncomfortable, and he escaped from them into the dim light of the adjoining room where there were no people, only a continuation of the row of solemn portraits on the wall.

'Our national heroes,' said someone behind him.

'I don't recognize them all,' he said. Paul had followed him unobserved.

'There are some of Aunt Kotie's family among them. If you're dead, you're a hero and then your portrait can be hung with all the others.'

'A whole Valhalla, a heaven full of heroes.'

'Now you're making fun of them.'

'I'm sorry.'

'You're mocking our ancestors, their trials and their struggles.'

'Is that a quotation?'

'Don't tell me that you weren't listening to Gerhard's speech!'

George laughed. 'I'm sorry, I didn't recognize the words.'

'You must talk about these people with respect,' said Paul. 'We have to be grateful to them. It's to them that we owe everything we have and are today.'

In the other room people were moving about, talking. The long table was pushed aside out of the way and the chairs were arranged along the walls. From where they were standing on the threshold between the two rooms, outside the circle of light cast by the lamps, George and Paul surveyed the activity.

'Uncle Wet's brought his accordion,' said Paul. 'He can hardly wait to begin.' They heard the first notes of the music, unrelated phrases rolling through the room and, above the hum of voices, a girl's laughter. 'Now they're going to dance.'

'Don't you dance?' George asked.

'Why should I?' He looked at them contemptuously, his hands in his pockets. 'Watch: Daniella's looking for Johannes.'

'How do you know?'

'I know them, don't I? Look — you've got a good view of what's happening from where we're standing. Gerhard's the first prize and Johannes the second. The other men are simply also-rans.'

'You're cynical,' said George.

'But it's true, you can see for yourself. The contest for Gerhard is between Aunt Loekie and her daughters, but the daughters move quicker and Aunt Loekie's already had too much to drink.'

George followed the movements of the people as they milled around in the lamp-light while Lourens provided snatches of music. 'We'd better join them,' said George, but Paul held him back.

'No. Wait a bit. Look, Danie's found Johannes: now at least she's satisfied.'

'You father is going to dance with Aunt Loekie.'

'She's not so young any more, but she's still a tasty morsel.'

'That's not very respectful.'

'But it's true. I'm not saying anything that isn't true.'

The dancers moved out into the middle of the room and the others withdrew towards the walls to watch, while Lourens struck up a quick old-fashioned dance-tune.

'Take your partners, folk, for the quadrille,' Paul whispered. 'Look at Aunt Loekie going round and round, look how she's dancing from one partner to the next, ready to be grabbed! From Pa to Johannes to Gerhard to late Uncle Frank, from father to son, she's gone the whole circuit.'

'What are you talking about?' asked George for Aunt Loekie and Hattingh were jogging around the room to the beat of the music and Paul's words had no relevance to the dancing.

'It's the Great National Quadrille,' said Paul. 'And there come the girls, Danie and Hannie and Hennie, following in mother's footsteps, along the beaten path — from Hendrik to Johannes to Gerhard to the next man.'

'Am I supposed to take all this seriously?' asked George.

'I tell you, I'm speaking the truth. I know them: you just have to watch and listen, then you know everything that's happening behind the door and under the blankets.'

At a distance the dancers circled in the lamplight; Hattingh and Aunt Loekie laughing and attracting attention with their dash and elegance, Mrs Hattingh a little unsteady as she was propelled by Raubenheimer's powerful elbow-movements, and the three young men with the Lourens girls. Next to him Paul's urgent whispering continued, almost lost in Lourens's accordion-playing.

'And there comes Gerhard, the king of the country, the prize stallion, the stud ram. Uncle Frank was a great lady's man in the district but they'd have trampled him underfoot to get to Gerhard.'

'You're saying more than you ought.'

'When Uncle Frank was alive, he spent more time at Eensgevonden than here at home. And when he went there, Aunt Loekie used to send Uncle Wet off in the truck to sit in the mealie-field for as long as Uncle Frank stayed — oh, it's a quick intricate dance we do here; we've got the world-record for changing partners: it's our very own achievement, our national boast...' He spoke louder with growing excitement.

'Careful — they'll hear you.'

'Look,' said Paul, gripping George's arm. 'Just look at Danie with Johannes. She'll have to get married one of these days, and Johannes is the best bet, if she can catch him. It's just as likely to be his child as anyone else's, even though Ma and Pa would rather not have one of the Lourens girls as a daughter-in-law.'

'I must go,' said George and shook Paul off.

'But I haven't told you everything yet.'

'I don't want to hear it. Why are you telling me such things?'

Paul was silent. 'Why are you so bitter? After all, these are your own people, your own family.'

'I'd like to destroy them,' said Paul slowly. 'I hate them.'

'Why?'

Paul was silent for a long time, so long that George assumed that he wasn't going to answer, and he was turning away towards the lamp-light and the dancers when Paul said: 'Because I love them. Because they hang on to me so that I can't escape: they're dragging me down with them. Help me!' he whispered and George looked at him astonished at his sudden intensity and anguish, but before he could say anything Carla came across the room to them.

'Why are you two here in the corner?' she asked.

'I came to look at the portraits,' said George, for Paul said nothing.

'They're looking for you. Everyone's asking where you are.'

'I'm coming.'

'What about you, Paul,' she said, in a gentle voice. 'Aren't you coming to dance?'

'Who is there to dance with?'

'You can dance with me; I haven't got a partner.'

'I can't dance with my sister.'

'There's cake and orange-syrup in the kitchen,' she said. 'Aunt Kotie would be glad of your help, to carry it in.'

'That's girls' work.' Paul walked away from them.

'Doesn't he like parties?' asked George.

'He's shy with people: he doesn't know what to say to them. Only how to make them angry. And they tease him: they've already teased him tonight about the shirt you lent him.'

'It seems that I, too, can't do anything right.'

'It's not your fault,' she said. She spoke pensively, as if she were unconscious of the people in the adjoining room, the voices, the shuffling feet, the sleepy waltz which Lourens was now playing.

'And you,' he asked, 'where did you disappear to?' She shrugged. 'It seems that you don't like parties either.'

'I'm another who doesn't know what to say to people.'

Together they returned to the brightly-lit room where the dancers were. 'Oh, there you are, Carla,' called Aunt Maria who was sitting at the side of the room, looking on.

'I was helping in the kitchen, Aunt, and then I had to go

and look for George and Paul: they'd both disappeared.'

'I'm glad. I was sitting here wondering who was helping Kotie in the kitchen. I thought I'd better go and see if I could lend a hand.'

'No, it's not necessary, Aunt Maria. You must stay where you are and watch the dancing. You really don't have to worry about anything.'

'And you, George. I was sitting at table looking at you all the time. You know, there are things you think you've forgotten about; you don't even know any more that they happened and then suddenly they come back. You remember it all again. Tonight I was thinking all the time about your family, your mother and your grandparents. It's very odd: in some ways you're a complete stranger to me and then suddenly it's as if I've known you all my life.' She looked grotesque as she sat there but when she held out her hand to him, he felt again how finely-formed, delicate and soft it was, and in her features he detected a purity of line which he had not expected, something which once more disarmed him and made it impossible for him to find her ludicrous.

'I'm so glad that you've come back and are here tonight. Anna Neethling was my god-daughter; I'm glad that I've been able to see her son.'

'I'm happy to be here, Aunt Maria,' he said, and stood next to her, with Carla, until the music came to an end.

'People, come and help yourselves!' called Aunt Kotie who was carrying in a tray of cold drinks and cake. Everyone came thronging to the table where she put it down. Already somewhat unsteady on her high heels, Aunt Loekie came to George with two glasses. 'What Kotie's got over there is only orange-syrup,' she said pressing a slopping glass of brandy into his hands, 'and that's for children. Come on, put away a glass of this and show us how you can dance!'

'I'll get a glass of orange-syrup for you, Aunt Maria,' said Carla and disappeared before George could offer to do it for her. He touched Aunt Loekie's glass with his and drank: he was already used to the harsh drink and it no longer burnt his throat or made his eyes water. He began to experience a sense of well-being, acquiescence, and a hazy expectation that this strange gathering of people mostly unknown to him could yet hold something for him.

Aunt Kotie poured orange-syrup for the girls and Gerhard went from one man to the next filling glasses with brandy. 'So, George,' he said, 'why is your glass still full?'

'I got here before you did, Gerhard,' said Aunt Loekie, but then one of her daughters called her over to whisper something excitedly. The cakes and orange-syrup had been served, the brandy poured, and people sat down. Glass in hand, accordion still hanging around his neck, Lourens wiped the sweat off his face and joked with Aunt Kotie.

'What! Don't tell me they've finished dancing already!' said Aunt Loekie indignantly, not listening to what her daughter was saying.

'Fanie's going to recite,' said Gerhard. 'He says you're interested in his poems, George.'

'He told me that he wrote poetry, but I haven't seen any of it. Is it good?'

Gerhard smiled. 'I know nothing about poetry: you mustn't ask my opinion. I only know that people like the verses he makes; sometimes they're roused by them, so at least they serve a useful purpose.'

'Must everything be of use?'

Gerhard was a bit taken aback by the question. 'What's the point of things which are of no use to anyone?'

'They can simply be beautiful: isn't that enough?'

Gerhard attached no importance, however, to this line of thought. 'Our life here is a serious matter. We have to fight to survive: there's no time for useless things.'

By now everyone was seated; only Raubenheimer remained standing before them, a little ill at ease, his toes turned out, his arms hanging at his sides. They were still whispering among themselves, and Aunt Miemie was loudly querulous about a cushion which had slipped down behind her back. Then everyone was quiet. Raubenheimer closed his eyes and slowly and solemnly raised an arm as he began.

'God of our fathers, once more we affirm
Our faith in Thee, where with bowed heads we pray,
Certain that Thou will raise us from the dust
And lead us forward to a brighter day ...'

'He wrote it himself,' Aunt Loekie hissed at George. 'He's always at it, making poems. He's the sort of person you'd be interested in.'

'Why so?' asked George.

'Someone who's a bit different. We're probably very uninteresting to you: there's nothing marvellous about farming people.' Her whispered words were not really a statement of fact: rather, they were a question, almost a plea to him to deny, to contradict them.

'A person doesn't have to write poems to be interesting,' he said, and she smiled at him over her glass.

'Ma, Ma...,' whispered her daughter behind her, and

she looked around impatiently. George hadn't followed the gist of Raubenheimer's poem: the teacher stood with his arm still upraised, pointing over the heads of his audience towards something infinitely distant.

>*'Civilization's torch, with brave and steady hand*
>*They bore across the void and darkling land . . .'*

he called to them. Who was he talking about, George wondered. Lourens tried to relieve himself of the weight of his accordion and in the silence the instrument squeaked suddenly and the girls giggled.

>*'Then clattered spears upon white wagon-hoods . . .'*

'Gerhard, while you're standing here with the bottle, pour us a little more.' Whispering, Aunt Loekie wasn't even pretending to listen.

'Aunt Loekie will make George altogether tipsy.'

'Agh, nonsense! A few drinks won't do him any harm. And then perhaps we'll see what's hidden underneath his good manners and smart clothes.'

'That'll be interesting,' said Gerhard, smiling, and once more filled George's glass although it was still half-full.

>*'Heroes were all — man, woman, child alike,*
>*No sacrifice withheld, no gift refused . . .'*

Raubenheimer's face was red with exertion or excitement and the veins in his temples were corded. His eyes were still closed and now his other arm was raised, too, stretched out as if in blessing or prophecy.

'I much prefer dance-music,' whispered Aunt Loekie.

'What do you say, Gerhard?'

'One can't always be dancing, Aunt Loekie.'

'No. If you had your way, there'd be no more music in the world.'

'Mommy!' Her daughter was still trying to gain her attention.

'My God, what's the matter with you then, Danie?' she asked impatiently. 'Can't you hear that Fanie's busy reciting a poem?'

It didn't matter if he got drunk, thought George, drinking again; that he'd completely missed half the poem wasn't important either. The room was beginning to seem a peaceful place in the lamp-light and in his ears was a droning in which from time to time Fanie's words were audible.

> *'In darkest night of nationhood, Thy voice*
> *Our leaders in their deep despair accosted . . .'*

'I used to love poetry, when I was a girl,' Aunt Loekie informed him. 'I could still recite something for you.' Then she noticed that he wasn't listening to her. 'What's the matter?' she asked.

'I'm waiting to hear what rhymes with "accosted",' said George.

'Oh, Fanie's poem!' she said and was quiet for a moment, reflecting.

> *'And whatever the battle we started to fight,*
> *Before we were halfway we'd lost it . . .'*

she recited in a whisper and laughed. Aunt Kotie and Mrs Hattingh turned around to look at her. 'Pardon me, I'm

sure,' she added in a more subdued voice to George and
Gerhard. 'But I'm impatient to get moving again. What
year of our history do you reckon Fanie's reached by
now?' She jolted George in the ribs with her elbow.
Gerhard was as little affected by her high spirits as he was
by the poem. Raubenheimer's voice boomed louder, his
hands rose above his head as if he wanted to draw
inspiration from heaven and his body followed: on tip-
toe he recited on and on, swaying backward and forward.

'Thy wisdom gave us light, Thy power led,
We neither strayed nor fell, nor shall we fail.
Hallowed our struggle and it will not end
Until the truth and justice of our cause prevail.'

There was silence and then the applause engulfed him.
He stood with bowed head, smiling, humble, exhausted,
accepting their homage while they crowded around him,
the seer, the bard, the prophet.

'Come on, let's dance,' said Aunt Loekie. Gerhard was
signalling to someone in the crowd. 'How about it,
George? We're already old friends — I don't have to wait
for you to ask me.'

'I don't think that George is much of a dancer,'
Gerhard said.

'Fortunately not everyone is as elevated above us
earthlings as you are, Gerhard,' she said somewhat tartly.
But just then Hendrik came up to her.

'What about it, Aunt Loekie: after all, it's my turn
now,' he said and before she realized what was
happening, he had borne her away; she was still clutching
her glass. George and Gerhard remained behind together
while Lourens picked up his accordion and began to

play again.

'Aunt Loekie seems to be enjoying the evening,' George said to break the silence.

'Most people enjoy an opportunity to get together like this on any pretext whatever. But unluckily I'm not one who cares for dancing and music and such things. I'm not suited to the goings-on here tonight.'

'I'm sorry then that I'm the cause of its being foisted on you. I'm to blame for the whole thing being arranged.'

'One does one's duty,' Gerhard said in a serious manner.

'I shall have to go and do mine. I haven't danced once yet this evening.'

'There's plenty of time for dancing. Everyone's going to spend the night here: they certainly can't leave before it's light.'

'You're already talking about leaving, George?' asked Johannes. Unnoticed, he had approached and was standing next to George, smiling.

'I must dance once at least.'

'You can talk a bit first. We've chanced on a peaceful spot here: no-one will come and bother us.'

They stood on either side of him and, through the rather pleasant haze encompassing him, he realized that they had him cornered, these two young men in their spotless white shirts, who, though they smelled of sweat and drink, still had complete control of themselves: they were sober, watchful, polite.

'Well, George, how do you like our part of the world?' asked Gerhard.

Again this question, so difficult to answer. 'It's . . . different,' he said. 'Different from what I expected.'

'In what way?'

'I knew it as my parents described it to me. I've been forgetting how much time has elapsed; I never realized that everything had changed.'

'Are you disappointed?'

'I am still trying to assimilate it.'

It was Gerhard who questioned him and kept the conversation going; Johannes, silent and smiling, stood and listened. Was he there as spectator, observer, witness or guard, George wondered, somewhat confused, and of what or of whom? The silent presence beside him made him uneasy.

'I hear you were at Rietvlei yesterday,' Gerhard said.

'Yes.'

'Then you've seen how they've destroyed it.'

'Yes.'

'And what do you feel about it?'

He considered telling Gerhard to mind his own business and putting an end to this unwished-for discussion, but he suppressed the inclination.

'A bit sad. I can still remember the farm as it used to be.'

Gerhard frowned: this was obviously not the answer he was expecting. 'And what are you going to do about it?'

'What do you mean?'

Gerhard gripped his arm and drew him a little farther to one side, deeper into the shadow at the end of the room where the light didn't reach. Johannes followed them. 'You came back to see the farm; after all these years and in spite of everything that's happened, you came back: it must still mean something to you. Rietvlei is now yours: what are you going to do with it?'

'Try and sell it.'

'Are you serious?'

'What else can I do with it? I can't stay here. I live

abroad, I work abroad: I must go back . . .'

'Did you undertake this whole journey for a visit of a few days?'

'Yes. Perhaps it was sentimental, but I wanted to see the farm once more, for the last time. You could call it a pilgrimage.'

Gerhard wasn't listening. 'Wouldn't you feel a traitor to your family if you were to sell it?'

'The farm was my grandparents' whole life, and my mother grew up there; she had her memories and she wanted to preserve this bond; however symbolic it might have been, she didn't ever consider severing it. But I have my own life and Rietvlei is no part of it. It belongs to my youth, and my youth is past.'

'You were born here. You can take up your life here where it was interrupted.'

'No. That's no longer possible: it was too long ago and meanwhile too much has happened. Nothing of what there was has survived unchanged.'

'The land is the same.'

'I am not a farmer, nor do I want to be one.'

'The country is the same.' Gerhard drew him still deeper into the shadow and spoke more softly and more urgently: the music had stopped and people were moving about in the room. 'The farm is important, but it's only a part of the whole: you don't have to work it. Do you feel nothing for the country?'

'It's become an alien land to me. It's only now and then that I recognize something, and every time it happens I'm startled.'

Gerhard was still frowning, his grey eyes searching, as if he were baffled. Yes, George thought again: they were cold eyes; the face was handsome but if one looked carefully, one could see a hardness, a total lack of human warmth in the features. From him one could expect no mercy.

Almost immediately Lourens began playing again, a sad, slow waltz. 'I must go,' George said once more but neither Gerhard nor Johannes moved aside to let him pass. 'I've discussed this already with Johannes,' George said, 'and I haven't changed my mind since.'

'We spoke only about farming,' said Johannes. 'We spoke about boreholes and tractors.'

'Are there then other possibilities?' George felt that if he did not go then and there he might lose his temper, but the brandy had made him lethargic, pacific; after all they probably didn't mean to be importunate: it was just that their way of doing things, their manner, was different from what he was accustomed to.

'There are several possibilities,' said Gerhard. 'We need men who love their country and their people, who are willing to dare much for them, to fight and if need be to die for them...'

'What are you proposing I should do?'

'Stay here.' Gerhard spoke softly, his face close to George's, his clear grey eyes fixed on him. 'You'll soon enough see what there is to do. All you need is courage and faith and tenacity.'

'And why should I give up everything I have to hazard all, here in a strange place?'

'Because you have a duty to your country, your people, your forefathers; there is a holy command laid on you which must be obeyed.'

' "Holiness" is a vague thing, and obedience doesn't mean blind submission. It's a question of choice: what you choose is that which you undertake voluntarily, willing the end. I've already made a different choice.' He spoke in a detached way, hardly mindful of Gerhard, but in any case it was clear that what he was saying was not getting through to him.

'Do you know how your grandparents ended their days?' Gerhard asked. 'They were driven away from their own farm like dogs to live in a back-room in town. And do you know what happened to your uncle, your mother's brother? Did they tell you? The police interrogated him for hours on end and beat him when he didn't want to answer. When he couldn't stand any more, he fell down and couldn't get up and a policeman kicked him to death.'

George looked at the impassive eyes. 'If you were a policeman interrogating a prisoner, you'd do the same,' he said and was shocked at his words. He really was drunk, he thought, and his voice, Gerhard's face next to his own, the music — all seemed equally remote, indistinct. Yet he really could feel Gerhard's fists pounding a defenceless body; Gerhard would kick and kick at the soft flesh, his face as grim and unmoved as it was now, his eyes showing no feeling. So that was how it had been: Uncle Kosie, the smiling young man in the photograph albums, had ended his life on a cement floor in his own blood and excrement.

'George!' Aunt Loekie called, forcing a way through the dancers. 'I've got you now, George, and we're going to dance. Your very first dance here, among your own people . . .' She pulled him on to the dance-floor: Gerhard and Johannes made no move to detain him. She flung her arms around him and they were borne away on the melancholy swell of the music.

'Why have you been making yourself scarce all

evening? If I'd known what a good dancer you were, I would have come to look for you ages ago.' He wasn't a good dancer at all, but she hardly knew what she was saying; automatically he guided her in time to the music. Johannes was also dancing, he saw, one of the Lourens girls clinging to him; Gerhard was dancing with Carla. With some satisfaction George noted that Gerhard danced badly, his movements stiff and awkward; Carla looked away over his shoulder expressionlessly, as if the dancing and the music didn't concern her.

'I don't know how Kotie can live like this, without electricity or anything. And then she makes you feel inferior because you've got such things. But she's such a dedicated self-sacrificing person, it's not surprising that poor Frank took to drink. He was drunk, of course, the day the police nabbed him: he was hanging around as usual in the bar in town instead of coming home, and who can blame him? And his tongue ran away with him.' She told him these things carelessly, not trying to lower her voice, and he was thinking just soberly enough to steer her away from that part of the room where Aunt Kotie and Hattingh were dancing.

'Wet can't be expected to play for them all night,' she added inconsequently. 'It's not that he minds, but they always expect him to do the dirty work for them just because he never says no to anybody. But they don't trust him: oh no, we're not supposed to know anything, we're not good enough . . .'

The music ended on a long-drawn-out note from the accordion, and Aunt Loekie broke off, forgetting what she was going to say. When he let her go, she was unsteady on her feet.

'Well done, George!' Hattingh called. 'Now we must

see you dance a real old-fashioned farm-dance. Come on, come and get yourself something to drink.'

'I was wondering where you were,' Bettie said, her unpowdered face shining with excitement and exertion. 'I thought you'd gone back to Germany.'

'Switzerland.'

'It's high time you joined in the dancing. I don't know why, but as soon as the music starts, all the men disappear. It's only Uncle Hennie who still takes pity on us. Fanie's also too bad when it comes to dancing.' Her last comment was added hastily for Fanie approached them with long strides and waving arms.

'Bettie, Aunt Miemie's calling you,' he said, but she went on talking as if she hadn't heard him.

'It's not all that often that we get a chance to dance on the farm, and then when someone like you comes who can dance, you disappear with all the other men to stand talking politics.' She was obviously waiting for an invitation as she stood there, beaming at him.

'Bettie, Aunt Miemie's calling you,' Fanie repeated. Bettie hesitated a little but she couldn't pretend not to have heard him: indeed, Aunt Miemie's voice reached them, shrill and imperative, from the other end of the room. Bettie shrugged impatiently and tripped away on her high heels to the old lady who had to be lifted to her feet from her chair with the support of Bettie and Mrs Hattingh and accompanied outside, step by step, slowly through the dancers.

'Well, are you enjoying the evening?' Raubenheimer asked. 'Tell me: what did you think of Gerhard's speech?' He lowered his voice to add confidentially: 'They say he speaks well, at any rate he thinks he does, but he's never made much of an impression on me. Naturally, he's an important man in the district: he always takes the lead and all the girls fancy him, but that's not everything. People always judge by externals, but they're not the most important things, are they? I believe . . .'

The teacher loomed above him. George saw only the white shirt and dark tie on a level with his eyes and heard the voice droning on above his head, interwoven with the music of the accordion. The collar of Fanie's shirt was frayed at the edges, the collar of his jacket discoloured and greasy. Suddenly he felt tired and antagonistic, and went to sit down without excusing himself. Fanie followed. There was no empty chair near his and Fanie was forced to remain standing, his face with the gleaming spectacles now far above George while he continued speaking, the gist of what he was saying being for the most part unintelligible. Gradually, talking all the while, he bent his head lower, and then his shoulders; his whole body bowed now from a great height, like a tree affording the relief of shade, like a man-eating plant stretching threatening tentacles towards its prey. '. . . the noblest there is . . .', heard George, '. . . a tiny handful among ordinary people . . . a loftier path . . .' What was he talking about? George wondered hazily as he sat looking at the dancers, glass in hand, and then he saw that the teacher was beginning to pull out a roll of papers from an inside pocket. 'You apparently care as little for dancing as I do,' he said, bent double, his mouth almost on George's forehead. 'Perhaps we can slip away unnoticed, and then I could read you a few little things. What you heard tonight was only a small piece for a particular occasion: these people like that sort of thing and I find their appreciation deeply moving, but there are more personal pieces which I couldn't show everybody, poems which

express the promptings of the heart, one might say ...'
He had a hand on George's shoulder and in his excitement
his lips fleetingly touched George's forehead.

'*Pax Domini sit semper vobiscum*,' George said to
himself and stretched out a hand to push Fanie gently
back. '*Et cum spiritu tuo*,' he responded to himself and
smiled as the words surfaced in his memory. Raubenheimer
hadn't understood.

Then he heard once more the approaching click of
Bettie's high heels. She had apparently handed Aunt
Miemie over to Mrs Hattingh's care and was making
purposefully for George.

'Fanie, Aunt Miemie says the children have to go to
sleep now,' she said without looking at Raubenheimer.

'They're not in anybody's way.'

'Aunt Miemie says you must see to it that they go to
bed at once. It's already after midnight.'

'Then let them go to bed. I'm not stopping them.'

'Aunt Miemie says that you personally must see to it
that they go to bed, otherwise they'll be up all night
getting into mischief.'

'And what about the girls? I'm not responsible for
them.'

'Aunt Miemie says you've got to see to the children.
I'm busy helping her in the bathroom.'

'You know that you're responsible for the girls.'

'Go and talk to Aunt Miemie about it, then.' The
discussion was over as far as she was concerned. Fanie
sought for a rejoinder, but didn't find one. He had hidden
the roll of papers behind his back at Bettie's approach,
and now he put it back into his pocket. 'We'll talk again,'
he said to George with a constrained smile, and slapped
him on the shoulder.

She called after him as he walked away: 'And Aunt Miemie says that you must see to it that the boys' room and the girls' room are on opposite sides of the passage, not next to each other.'

'But where is Aunt Miemie then, Bettie?' Aunt Kotie asked. 'Can she manage?'

'Yes, Aunt Kotie, Aunt Mart is with her.'

'Oh, that's fine. Then perhaps you could help Carla to cut up the cakes and hand them around. You don't mind, do you?'

'No, Aunt,' Bettie said submissively but she flounced off, impatiently as before, and her hips, swinging in a dress too short and skimpy for them, expressed reluctance and indignation.

The waltz continued: Aunt Loekie had disappeared, but her daughters all had partners, Danie still clamped in Johannes's arms — or perhaps he in hers. Was the whole evening, George thought, going to pass like this for him: imprisoned in a corner while one guest after the other seized upon him?

'We're not really giving you a chance to dance,' said Aunt Kotie as if she divined what he was thinking.

'I don't much care for dancing, Aunt Kotie.'

She smiled. 'Just like Gerhard. He does it because he's obliged to, even if it's Carla he's dancing with. And his father so loved dancing!' George looked at her pleasing, regular profile, the determined mouth and chin, the straight nose and broad forehead, and then she looked at him with Gerhard's clear grey eyes. 'But we're all so eager to talk to you: that's why we pounce on you all the time.'

'I'm glad to have the opportunity to get to know the people here.'

'Your own people: yes, I can understand that. I only

wish that there were still members of your immediate family here, George. Of your mother's family. Can you still remember them?'

'Only my grandparents and not very clearly at that. I remember my grandmother best.'

'She was a wonderful woman — there wasn't anyone in the district who could create a garden like she could. In her time Rietvlei was a real show-place. And now . . .'

The music stopped again. Lourens propped his accordion against a chair, had a drink, and wiped his face. Aunt Miemie had not returned; the school-children, who had sat subdued in a corner of the room the whole evening, looking on, were being led away by Fanie. The room looked deserted, dominated by the figure of Aunt Maria who sat alone, with folded hands.

'Come with me,' Aunt Kotie said, taking a lamp from the table. She preceded him through the adjoining room where he and Paul had looked at the portraits, across the passage and through other rooms. He couldn't see where they were: the rooms they traversed were swallowed up in darkness, and only the portraits on the walls were visible, lit by the lamp Aunt Kotie raised as she walked past them, as if she were looking for something. He saw bearded faces, clean-shaven faces, yellowing studio-portraits and photographs of gatherings of all sorts, framed against the white walls.

'Look,' she said halting at one of them. 'It's here. Can you see? That's your mother and her brother, Kosie, and those are your grandparents. It was taken in front of the church on our wedding-day.'

Aunt Kotie, a bride with her hair in tight curls, in layers of veiling and bedecked with bows and flowers; a handsome, laughing young man at her side on the little steps of a church and both of them flanked by people in their best clothes. He bent to look closely at the faces she was pointing out to him. They were half-hidden by the shoulders and heads of others; he saw little but the reflection of the lamp in the glass covering the photograph.

'It was winter,' Aunt Kotie said. 'You can see that by the clothes the people are wearing. A lovely winter's day — cold and clear. Sometimes I think that these days we don't get the lovely winter weather we used to.'

'Was my mother already married?' he asked, for something to say.

'No. It was just before her own wedding. And she wasn't married here, it was somewhere else, and only her own family was present. But I still remember well what she wore at our wedding: a blue coat and a blue velvet hat. She looked beautiful: she was always so well-dressed. . .' Scarcely-perceptible features, a head half-averted, a hand — was it indeed his mother? He remembered how she would turn her head to stare at the mountains, and cry out that they were hemming her in.

Aunt Kotie walked on, stopping at every photograph to tell George something about the people on it. Her voice dispassionate, she told him of murder, manslaughter, violence; she bore herself erect and there was no tremor of the hand holding the lamp. On she went, like a guide shepherding tourists in a palace long untenanted, or under the vaulting of a church, past murals, altars and relics. The rooms were empty, bleak, cold, and their footsteps echoed on the bare boards; a beadle with a clanking bunch of keys, an aged sacristan, a nun with lowered eyes displaying old treasures and elucidating arcane matters, Sebastian pierced with arrows, Lawrence lapped about in flames, Barbara kneeling to receive the blow of the sword; a lowered voice, the glow of candles before an image, and the faint, distant smell of incense. . .

Kotie's voice recalled him. 'The things in this house are priceless: no money can buy them. I know you understand that, George.'

He nodded: no words were appropriate. There was absolute silence, as if they were alone in the house. Neither voices nor music penetrated to where they were.

'I knew all these people,' Aunt Kotie said. 'I was involved in it all, in the whole struggle, I myself participated. . .'

Behind her a door swung open soundlessly without her noticing it or being aware that George was looking past her into the darkness. In the light of the lamp he saw something move, and then realized that it was Johannes, his shirt unbuttoned, and Danie looking over her shoulder, her eyes bright in the tousled hair falling over her face. Her arm appeared, pulling Johannes back into the darkness and the door closed as silently as it had opened. Aunt Kotie was still speaking. Had he really seen the two of them? So swiftly, so noiselessly had it happened that he began to doubt it.

'What matters is that it shouldn't be forgotten,' she said. 'Sometimes I feel that I have a solemn duty to see to it that these things are preserved, and to remind people of what has happened. Some of them don't want to be reminded, there are some who haven't kept faith, and young people who don't even attach importance to such things . . .' She sighed. 'And that, above all, is why your return means so much to me.'

'I'm afraid that my motives were entirely selfish.'

'It doesn't matter: what's important is that you're here.'

They walked back along the passage, Kotie lighting their way with the lamp, and once more he heard the sound of music in the distance. She opened the door to the living-room. 'Now you must tell me about your mother, George.'

'Kotie!' summoned Aunt Miemie, now back in their midst, and Kotie had to put down the lamp and go to her.

'Come on, George, where's your glass?' called Hattingh. 'Come, let me fill it up for you again, man. You must drink and enjoy yourself. We've hardly seen you dance yet. Don't try to tell me you're shy!' He laughed boisterously and walked off, before George could answer, to slap Gerhard on the shoulder and, lowering his voice, began to tell him a joke.

'Hell, but a chap gets hot from all this playing!' said Lourens. 'Let's have a drink together, George. It's not every day that I can drink with someone who's come from abroad.' It was quite obvious that he'd already had too much to drink: his speech was slightly slurred. 'And so — how do you like our style of party? Good food, good music, a few glassfuls and a house full of people. Some pretty girls here, eh?' He edged a little nearer. 'And a nice big house to play hide-and-seek in, eh? Sometimes a person feels just like that sort of game, am I right?' He laughed and tried to dig George in the ribs, but his aim was bad and he staggered a little. 'Well, never mind, you're young . . . you don't have to say a word . . . I understand.' George remained silent.

Mrs Hattingh joined them. 'You must be tired by now, Wet.'

'Tired? Never! I'm full of beans, just look at me: I'm

livelier than most of the youngsters here.'

Mrs Hattingh looked anxiously around the room. 'Yes, as far as my children are concerned, I don't know what to say. Now it's Johannes who's disappeared. . .'

'For goodness' sake, Mart, why do you still worry yourself about them? Come and sit next to me: we can talk a bit.'

'I'm sleepy,' she said. 'I can't stay up late any more like I used to.'

George walked away from them. The room had emptied: some people had disappeared; those who remained were quiet. It certainly was late, and he wondered if it were possible to go somewhere and sleep.

Two of the Lourens girls confronted him: these must be Hannie and Hennie, he thought. He saluted them solemnly with a raised glass and a bow. They giggled, but made no attempt to move aside: it seemed rather as if they wanted to bar his way, standing before him with linked arms.

'What can I do for you?' he asked, and they giggled again, nudging each other and whispering.

'We wondered why you don't dance,' said one of them.

'You've only danced once tonight,' said the other.

'And with our ma. . .'

'Don't you like dancing?'

'It's not right. All the young men have disappeared and we're left sitting here. . .'

They hesitated, looking at one another. 'Will you dance with us?' one said in a rush, and both burst out laughing.

'With which of you?'

'With both.'

'But first with me: I'm older than she is.'

'And the next dance with me, then.'

'Look, Dad's going to play again. Agh, please, Daddy,' she called, 'play us a waltz!'

She drew him towards her as the music began, and he felt her body against his, Hannie or Hennie, whichever of the two she was. She was probably a schoolgirl still — perhaps fifteen or at most sixteen — but the ripeness of her body was that of a woman's and she stared at him provocatively, her lips slightly parted. He was enveloped in the softness and warmth of that body and its scent of youth and sweat.

'I'm sorry,' he said. 'I don't dance very well.'

'You dance well enough,' she said, her intent look unaltered.

'It's too late: I ought to be going to bed.'

Aunt Loekie was approaching them across the dance-floor and heard his last words. 'Yes,' she said, 'it is so, it's time we all went to sleep. Why are you two pestering George? Haven't you already danced enough tonight?'

'No,' said one of the girls sulkily, but Aunt Loekie didn't hear her. 'Come on, leave the grown-ups alone. Rather go and look for Danie. Heaven knows where she's disappeared to.' With a gesture she chased them away as if they were chickens, and then took hold of George's arm herself. 'I've seen precious little of you tonight, you know. You've probably been busy with more important things — or more important people. I must still have a dance with you, but not now, it's too late.' She pulled him down next to her on a chair and yawned. 'Just look at Aunt Maria, sitting there like a statue. Why on earth doesn't she go to bed? And old Aunt Miemie — just in the way here, and spoiling everyone's pleasure. . .'

'Aunt Miemie's fallen asleep,' he said.

'Then she should also go to bed. She's only staying up to see what's happening, so that she'll have something new to gossip about.'

'That's probably all she has to keep her occupied.'

'You're telling me.' She stared at what remained of the drink in her glass. 'If I were to tell you everything that the old woman has managed to do in this district without setting foot outside her house. . .' She sat up straighter and began to talk with more energy, aroused by the subject. 'Oh yes, she's supposed to be in bad health, but it's all her imagination if you ask me. I've gone through worse things than she has — if I had to tell you. . . but I'm still very much alive: you just have to look at me. She does everything just to attract attention. . .'

He was beginning to yawn himself. 'One can understand it, at her age,' he said in a feeble attempt to calm Aunt Loekie, but she barely heard him.

'What does she really know about suffering? I myself went through all the troubles; we trekked here through it all. . . But you don't know about all that, do you? We didn't live here on the farm when we were first married,' she told him. 'I would never have married a farmer in a thousand years. Wet worked in the city; he was a foreman with thirty kaffirs working under him, we had a beautiful home, everything — I'm telling you I'm used to better things than this. But then the troubles began and everything was in a hell of a mix-up. The factory closed, our neighbour's house was burned down, and Wet decided that the best thing to do was just to come to the farm: it was the safest thing for us, and his father wasn't getting any younger anyway. And then at least we would all be together. So that was that: we packed all our belongings and put them on a hired lorry and got the hell out of there.'

George wasn't even trying to follow the adventures of Uncle Wet and Aunt Loekie. No-one was dancing any more, but Lourens was sitting playing quietly to himself, some little unrecognizable melody, no more than a faint melancholy ripple in the stillness of the room. His eyes were closed and he leaned back with his head against the wall. Aunt Miemie was indeed sleeping, still holding her walking-stick, and Aunt Maria was apparently also asleep.

'And there I was, sitting on our trunks as if I were guarding them,' Aunt Loekie was saying. 'My God, I could have saved myself the trouble, none of our things ever got to the farm, I never saw any of them again. My clothes, even my handbag with our money, and our engagement-ring, three diamonds. . .' She jerked herself awake again. 'There I'm sitting,' she resumed, 'and it was so dark that a whole rifle commando could have been standing in front of me and I wouldn't have seen a thing. But I listened carefully in case anything was approaching on the road. . .'

He would open the windows, if he were at home in Switzerland now with his friends, thought George, and get rid of some of the cigarette-smoke. The curtains would lift gently in the night air. The glow of scattered lamps, music in the background, and the lights of the city stretching away in the darkness — why had he come here, wasting time and money for the sake of a senseless journey and a visit that served no purpose? Otherwise he could now have been at home, at peace, with a few friends who'd stayed on after the others, sitting and smoking, listening to music, Lully or Rameau. His mother was dead and her house had still to be put to rights; why hadn't he rather stayed to do that? In his large room while the music sounded, the evening air would drift in, cool and clear, for over there it was Spring.

'. . .he hit me across the face, but I dodged and grabbed a crow-bar. . .' George opened his eyes, bemused. What was this woman talking about, sitting on the edge of her chair, her legs crossed and a glass in her hand, obligingly keeping a conversation going with a stranger at a party? '. . .and then he fell to his knees and blood was running into his eyes. . .' How had he got entangled in all this? What insanity it was for him to be scratching around here among slivers and shards, among gravel and ash, as if he were expecting to find something, a pebble, perhaps, or a button, a piece of scorched bone which could still be identified as a thigh-bone or jaw? Was he out of his mind? But Aunt Loekie, unperturbed, was continuing her saga, aroused and laughing at her recollections. 'Five times that night!' she cried out. 'And when the fifth one came. . .'

Carla was standing before them. 'Are you coming for coffee, George?' she said. 'Aunt Loekie, there's coffee.'

Aunt Loekie, in full spate, straightened up. Impatiently she said, 'Yes, yes. All right.'

'I'm coming,' said George. He hadn't even noticed that Carla and Aunt Kotie had brought in the coffee and cups. One by one, those who had disappeared began to return to get their coffee. Mrs Hattingh woke Aunt Miemie up.

'Shall we go and drink coffee?' asked George, but there was no response from Aunt Loekie until he stood up.

'She thinks she's already the mistress here,' she muttered, 'but she'll get more than she bargains for at Kommando Drift. Perhaps it seems a wonderful prospect to be Gerhard's wife and of course he's a goodlooking man, but she'll yet shed bitter tears over him; I know what I'm talking about.' She was tired, her face red and puffy, and there were tears in her eyes. 'And to be Kotie's daughter-in-law — no, that's too much of a price to pay just to get Gerhard into one's bed. . .' She hadn't noticed that George was walking away from her.

'And are you enjoying the evening?' Paul asked him.

'I can't even ask you the same question: as soon as you'd eaten you saw to it that you vanished.'

Paul handed him a cup of coffee, without answering. 'Are you enjoying yourself?' he repeated. 'Have you danced much? You're not looking very cheeful.'

'I've drunk too much and I'm dead-beat.'

'Do you want to go to bed?'

'Yes. I want to sleep.' It was so late that no-one could take offence if he disappeared now.

'Come,' said Paul. 'Then we can lie and talk a bit still.'

'Aren't you sleepy?'

'You're leaving tomorrow morning. There are lots of things I want to talk to you about.'

'Goodness, Paul! Where have you suddenly appeared from?' Mrs Hattingh had joined them. 'I've been looking for you all night — I even sent Hendrik outside to look in the car for you. What will people think of you? Such rudeness. . .' She spoke heatedly but kept her voice down so that no-one would hear her.

'George, have you had coffee yet?' Aunt Kotie asked, coffee-pot in hand. She looked tired but was serene and smiling as she moved about among her guests. 'Another cup, Johannes? Wet, don't you want any?' Wet, his eyes closed, was still playing sad, random snatches of music. The girls stood talking in a corner. Raubenheimer clasped his cup in both hands, yawning.

'Come and sit down,' Carla said to George and he sat

next to her and Aunt Maria.

'Aren't you coming to bed?' Paul asked.

'I'm coming: I just want to drink my coffee.'

'Aunt Loekie's cross because I interrupted your conversation,' said Carla. 'She's always delighted to find someone who hasn't yet heard her stories.'

'I couldn't even follow what she was telling me. Something about what happened to them on their way here from the city.'

'She always exaggerates: her experiences were no worse than anyone else's. But she doesn't really care about what happened to her, just as long as she can attract attention.'

As she sat there, hands folded on her vast bosom, Aunt Maria unexpectedly laughed; George hadn't thought she was listening.

'You sound as cynical as Paul,' he said.

'One gets so tired of all the self-pity and the dramatics. To you, of course, it's all new and perhaps it makes an impression, but if you've lived with it for years, you lose patience with it.'

'You're too severe, child,' said Aunt Maria. 'You people are young, you're still full of hope and courage. And so you're cruel sometimes, even though you don't mean to be.'

'Sometimes it's necessary to be cruel, Aunt,' said Carla, but her voice was gentler.

'Perhaps. But it hurts all the same. We've lived through a lot, child: we've been hard hit, we've fallen a long, long way.'

'Like a shooting star,' Carla murmured. 'Like dead leaves in the wind. It's past.' She was talking to herself, but then she leaned forward to take the old lady's hand.

There was something like a surging movement among

the guests. 'What's the matter?' George asked.

'Perhaps Aunt Loekie's been roused from the dead,' said Paul, who was sitting on the floor at George's feet, and George saw that Aunt Loekie was indeed, with renewed vigour, moving around, pushing and pulling this one and that, organizing something.

'God! I hope she's not going to try to organize folk dancing, is she?' said Carla.

'She's going to make the girls sing! I'm off to bed,' said Paul, jumping up.

The three Lourens girls had indeed been herded together by their mother in the middle of the room. Sleepy, shy, reluctant, they stood together while their father played an introduction on the accordion. Then they began to sing.

'I'm waiting on the hillside
Where the sweet proteas grow,
And I'm listening for your foot-step
Because I love you so. . .'

Their voices weren't quite pure: they were like bells which no longer had a perfect tone, but as they stood there together, in their white dresses, they looked young and vulnerable. George glanced at Carla sitting next to him, her hand still holding Aunt Maria's, her head resting against the old lady's shoulder. He saw that she wasn't listening.

'Are you and Gerhard engaged?' he asked softly.

'Where did you hear any such thing?'

'From Aunt Loekie.'

'Oh, Aunt Loekie. . .' She shrugged. 'People talk a lot: don't believe everything you hear.' Her mood had suddenly changed, and she was once more remote and disinclined to talk.

'And still I think with longing. . .'

the girls sang, and he heard the wistful melody of the accordion, noises far off in the depths of the night, people whispering to one another, a creaking chair, a moth flapping against a lampshade, and the barking of dogs somewhere — in a back-room, perhaps, or an outbuilding. He remembered that the dogs had barked that evening on their arrival, but after that he hadn't heard them again.

The music broke off suddenly. 'What's happening?' he asked but no-one answered. The men sprang to their feet and chairs went toppling; Gerhard ran to the door, Hendrik and Johannes following him. The girls were still standing in the middle of the room, startled. The barking of the dogs grew to a frenzy as if they were straining to get free and attack. Suddenly there was silence and then he heard people screaming and the tramp of heavy boots in the passage. 'What's the matter?' he asked.

Carla had also got to her feet, and stared at the door, gripping Aunt Maria's hand. 'It's the police,' she said.

He saw strangers entering, hustling Gerhard and the other men before them; he saw the uniforms, the holsters, the guns. One of them pushed Gerhard with such force that he fell, but he said nothing, and didn't try to defend himself. Before him, George saw a sketchy series of events, like an old movie flickering: people make jerky gestures; lips moved, but seemed to make no sound. Boots thudded on the bare floor-boards, there was continuous confused shouting; he heard the tinkle of breaking glass, and realized that it was Gerhard, Hendrik and Johannes who were being shouted at, and that they were making no response. Someone in uniform confronted him, but he could barely grasp what the man was saying or answer or find his passport to show to his interrogator. If he hadn't drunk so much, perhaps he could have said or done something, perhaps taken some action, but as it was he could only look on. The man who seemed to be in charge of the group strode across the room and came to a halt in front of Raubenheimer. George couldn't quite see what was happening but suddenly the man struck the teacher across the face so that he toppled and fell, slowly and silently like someone moving under water. The police who had remained standing at the door laughed, but George only saw their wide-open mouths: he could distinguish no sound.

No-one moved. Then the police turned and went as unexpectedly as they had come, taking Gerhard, Hendrik and Johannes with them.

Those who remained were still motionless, until one of the Lourens girls burst into shrill uncontrollable sobbing. He saw Carla's white face, Aunt Miemie stretching out trembling hands, Hattingh, his arm around his wife. Bettie was kneeling before Raubenheimer and with her tiny handkerchief carefully wiping the blood from his face.

'Those are blood-stains, George,' said Aunt Kotie: 'That's human blood on this cloth,' and she pressed it into his hands. He felt cold, and it was still pitch-dark. Had she really said it? He tried to remember, and then became aware of Paul lying next to him. He'd been dreaming.

He slept restlessly; short confused dreams succeeded one another fitfully. Only at dawn, just before Hattingh came to call them, he fell into a deeper sleep.

The sea-shore of his dreams was, as it always was, under a leaden sky, and dunes hid the hinterland. He ran across the beach, calling and calling, but the wind snatched away his words and he couldn't hear them. Would he never get up the loose sand of the dunes? He was panting, desperate, with the wind in his ears: then suddenly there was silence. He saw the white house before him and a path along which the women were walking away from him. Yes, of course, there was the white building with turrets and balconies and a broad verandah: a holiday cottage perhaps, or a hotel — he couldn't remember any more. With a cry of joy he recognized it and the women walking away looked around and stood waiting for him to catch them up.

Perhaps the sun would break through and put the clouds to flight: perhaps the weather would be fine. Every day of his visit he had expected it, and every day been disappointed, so that without much hope he looked out at the patchy sunshine of the grey morning and the spurts of windblown dust.

'I feel I owe you an apology for what happened there,' said Hattingh. 'Or at any rate for the fact that you were dragged into it. We wanted to welcome you, make you feel at home. . .'

'It's rather I who should apologise,' George said. 'It was on my account that we were all at Kommando Drift: if it hadn't been for me perhaps it would never have happened.'

'Oh, they would have got the boys in any case: it was just by chance that they could get them all in one swoop, because we were together. Otherwise they would have dragged them from their beds by night: that's the time they come, late at night, just before dawn. I can't tell you how often I've woken in fright: at every little sound you wake and think you can hear a car in the yard, or someone at the window. And we're watched all the time: they even knew we'd all be at Kommando Drift last evening. That's the way we live here — at their mercy. They can do with us what they like.'

'But Gerhard and the others will surely be charged and tried? If they've done nothing, they can't be held prisoner.'

'They can hold us or let us go; they can kill us or let us live. They don't have to answer for anything.'

'Is such a thing possible?'

'That's how we live. What can we do about it?'

Hattingh obviously needed to talk as he sat there, hunched up at the kitchen table, his hands folded. His wife shuffled back and forth in the kitchen, saying nothing.

The whole morning had passed in silence; even their departure from Kommando Drift had taken place virtually without a word. Conversation broken off in mid-sentence was not resumed; the song remained unfinished; about the events of the night before there was silence, as if they had never taken place. All that recalled them was the scattered litter in the main room, where Aunt Kotie was already beginning to tidy up, her eyes bright in her pale face: glasses, splinters of glass, dirty ashtrays, crumpled paper napkins, a chair knocked over, a torn portrait; the flag had been ripped off the wall. The guests had embraced and taken leave of one another without words, and George realized afresh that he was an outsider faltering to find words for things which these people accepted in silence. They had gone away, leaving the two women alone in the house at Kommando Drift.

In silence they had driven back, behind the truck in which the schoolchildren huddled together like frightened birds. In the same silence they had taken leave of the Moedersgift people. Raubenheimer had pressed George's hand, looking at him in a preoccupied way through the cracked lenses of his spectacles: he could see just as little with them as without them, and Bettie had to lead him by the hand. Aunt Miemie, sitting in the front of the truck, was a shrunken little figure whose jaws ceaselessly moved, and when George came to say goodbye to her, she turned her head away: she didn't want to look at him.

Hattingh had taken the Moedersgift people home.

Now he sat with Hattingh at the kitchen table, as Mrs Hattingh shuffled around behind them. 'Three of our finest young men,' said Hattingh. 'They were our hope for the future: they were everything that was young and strong and brave among us. . .' His voice broke.

'Daddy. . .' said his wife, busy with something at the cupboard, and after a while he regained control of himself.

'I'm sorry, George,' he said, 'but it's a heavy blow at our time of life.'

'Daddy,' Mrs Hattingh said, 'it's time that George started getting ready to leave.'

'Is there nothing I can do for you? I can't just leave you behind like this.'

'No. Nothing. There's nothing you can do,' said Hattingh. 'We've kept you here long enough. You mustn't miss your train. I should think you'll be glad to get away.'

'I've made you some sandwiches, George, and put some dried peaches in with them,' said Mrs Hattingh. 'Then at least you'll have something to eat on the train.'

He still hesitated, but took the packet from her. 'Thank you,' he said. 'I have to pack my suitcase, but I don't need much time for that.'

'Now you, too, are going,' she said. Her voice was flat, her eyes red with weeping. 'It feels as if I'm losing the last of my children.'

'Carla and Paul are still here.'

'Yes,' she said, but didn't sound comforted.

He needed only a few minutes to repack the few things he had taken out of the suitcase during his brief visit but he was glad of an excuse to withdraw to his room: he was helpless in the face of the grief of these two old people.

While he was busy, there was a knock on his door and Paul slipped in, swiftly closing the door behind him.

'Well,' he said, 'are you going?'

George nodded and the boy came to sit on his bed as he had done the night before, to watch him pack. 'I've still got your shirt,' he said.

'It doesn't matter. Keep it.'

Paul didn't reply but his face was flushed and reproachful. Then, when George bent to close the suitcase, he stretched out his arm and grasped George's wrist.

'Take me with you.'

'Where to?'

'Overseas. Away from here.'

'What would you do overseas?'

'I don't know: it doesn't matter. I just want to get away.' He leaned forward and spoke agitatedly. 'You saw what happened last night; I don't want it to happen to me — I don't want to end my life like Gerhard and the others, I don't want to become like Pa or Uncle Wet or Fanie with his poems. Help me get away!'

Taken aback by his vehemence George tried to free his hand but Paul's grip tightened. 'You can drive with me to town,' George said. 'Come with me as far as the city. . .' but Paul interrupted him.

'No: that's not far enough. They could still catch me any time.'

'Who?'

'The police. People. This life. . . I must go so far that they can't drag me back into all this, ever again.' With his hand still clutching George's arm desperately he slipped from the bed to his knees. 'It's the only chance I'll ever have, you've got to help me. Help me, help me — I tell you I'm afraid, afraid.' In his terror he clung to George's arm and began to weep quietly.

George tried to calm him. 'It's not possible. You know it's not. You probably haven't even got a passport. You can't just leave the country like that. You can't forsake you parents, alone as they now are. . .'

'Help me,' Paul repeated faintly, his head hanging. 'Help me: I can't go on, not like this.'

'Here you are,' said George, looking in his wallet for notes. 'Perhaps you can do something with this, I don't know. . .' It's all the cash I've got, he thought, while he pressed it into Paul's hand in the hope of calming him. It worked. The tears were still wet on his cheeks and his mouth was twisted but, kneeling there next to the bed, Paul stared at the money and his fingers automatically closed over it.

George turned away from him and went to stand at the window, lighting a cigarette. 'I have to go,' he said softly: 'I have to catch the train.'

Far away the sun shone over the veld and the blue-gum trees quivered in the wind. Somewhere on the other side of a barn someone began to chop wood; the thud of the axe was the only sound in the calm of the morning. Life was going on.

Paul stood up and wiped his eyes with the hand in which he clutched the crumpled notes; when George touched him in a gesture of farewell, he made no response, and looked at him as if he didn't see him.

George closed his suitcase and walked past Paul, through the kitchen where the Hattinghs were still together in their grief and their silence, and across the yard to the place behind the barn where Carla was chopping logs. She had once more put on her khaki clothes and she stood there with her back to him, so engrossed in her job that she neither saw nor heard his approach. He stood a while watching her, and then she became aware of him.

'I'm going now,' he said.

'Yes.' She pushed her hair back from her forehead.

'I'm sorry. . .' he began but she dismissed his sympathy with an abrupt movement of her hand.

'You don't have to say anything. Rather just go.'

But he remained, waiting, even though it was plain that she had no wish to start a conversation.

'What had they done?' he asked.

'It's not necessary to do anything. We're guilty simply because we exist.'

'Why were only those three taken away? There must be some reason and you're the only one who'll tell me.'

She considered her answer carefully before she spoke. 'They were plotting,' she said eventually, with great reluctance. 'They were trying to collect weapons.'

'I didn't know that such things were still being done.'

'Well then, you've learnt something in the last few hours before your departure, haven't you? People have been busy with such things for years, for as long as I can remember. That's all that's left to us, attempts like these.'

'Is that why Rietvlei was destroyed?'

'What makes you think that Rietvlei has anything to do with it?'

'Why else would the army be brought in to blow up an abandoned farmhouse?'

Once more she thought carefully before answering. 'It was used as a place where people hid, years ago, just after the old people left, and they also hid weapons there. It was a huge rambling house with lots of hiding-places. There was even a cellar.'

As far as she was concerned she had answered his question and she waited for him to go, but he still stood there. 'Is that how you came to know the farm? Is that how you knew about the roses and the dam?'

'Haven't you learnt yet that it's better not to ask questions?'

'I go on hoping that I'll get an adequate answer to one of my questions.'

'And when you know the answer — then what?'

'Perhaps it'll help me to understand.'

She walked away from him and sat down on a pile of logs. 'Once they took a wounded man there and there was no-one who could stay with him. So they asked me. That was the last time that I'd been to Rietvlei until I went there with you.'

'Tell me about it.' At first he thought that she was going to refuse, but then she began to speak in a very business-like way, as if she were relating something which barely concerned her.

'Johannes took me there one night. There was no moon and we walked across the veld; it's only a few hours on foot. They were to fetch him the following night: I spent the next day alone with him.'

'That must have been dangerous.'

'Of course, very dangerous, but I didn't care. There has to be something which means so much to you that you'll risk your whole life for it, that you'll risk everything for it.'

'Like what?'

'I don't know. I used to know but one changes and then one can't go on believing in the same things.'

He looked at the averted head with its cropped hair. 'Tell me about the house,' he said.

His question seemed to surprise her. 'The homestead at Rietvlei? It was a large house with lots of big rooms. Like Kommando Drift. A long passage with rooms on either side, and huge fireplaces. But it was quite empty: there was nothing left of what had been there before. Only in the room where we were there were a few boxes and mattresses on the floor. It must have been the larder: you could still see where there'd been shelves on the walls. It had advantages as a hide-away: there were two doors, so that one could easily escape. I stayed there with the man and the next night Johannes and some others came to fetch him. That's all there was to it.'

'Weren't you afraid?'

'No, I don't know why; perhaps I was too young and foolish. There was reason enough to be afraid, alone in an abandoned house with a delirious man. There were candles but I wasn't allowed to light them — in any case I didn't have any matches. So when it got dark I could only sit there with a blanket wrapped round me and wait for Johannes to return.' She was playing with a splinter of wood and suddenly laughed. 'And just before daybreak and again in the evening before it was altogether dark, I crept through the garden to get water from the dam; through the plants and shrubs, and branches of rose-bushes clutched at my clothes. That's how I knew about the dam.'

'And afterwards they came and annihilated the place.'

'A few months later the police raided it. Three of our people were hiding there, with lots of ammunition in the cellar. They refused to surrender but the place was surrounded. They held out for a few hours, but eventually all three were shot dead, in the kitchen. It was a huge room with a cement floor and their blood trickled across the floor into the passage. People spoke for a long time about the blood creeping across the floor: they still haven't forgotten it. Fanie wrote a poem about it.' She smiled fleetingly, and shook her head. 'They were still young, three young men like Gerhard and Johannes and Hendrik. Shot dead, there on the kitchen floor.'

He said nothing. 'But you're not really interested, are you?' she asked. 'All that interests you is the house in which your grandparents lived, your mother, your family, when they still owned the world and reigned over it, the earth and the whole firmament. But it was blasted to bits: there was hardly one stone left standing on another. The soldiers came with dynamite and blew up the whole house, blew up the dam, ploughed up the garden. It's a thing of the past, do you understand?' She spoke vehemently, almost tauntingly.

'I know it belongs to the past. But it meant something; it still means something.'

'The lives of those three boys also meant something, and their deaths meant something, but what are we to do about it? We must go on with our lives.'

'Aunt Maria was right,' he said. 'You're severe; you're cruel.'

She looked at him with her clear gaze. 'Do you want to add anything?' she asked.

'Unyielding, implacable. . .'

'Anything else?'

'Is that what you're trying to be?'

'How do you think it's possible to live here unless one's hard and relentless?' she asked but there was no harshness in her voice. Suddenly she bent her head and covered her face with her hands.

'Have I hurt you?'

She shook her head. 'One must be able to talk freely. One must be able to say these things. You can't carry them around with you and say nothing.'

'How can you bear to live like this?'

'Duty, love, habit — I don't know. It's how I grew up; these people are my people. But sometimes one has to be able to talk to someone; I told you that yesterday.'

'Is there anyone here you can talk to?'

'Paul, perhaps. He doesn't understand; he doesn't know himself exactly what he wants, but he at least listens without judging.'

'What will become of you?' She looked up.

'Does it bother you?'

'You can't go on like this, it's impossible to live this way. . .'

'If you have to you can do almost anything.'

'You must try to get away. . .'

She laughed. 'How?'

There was a long silence. Then he said: 'You can come with me.'

She didn't realize immediately what he meant. 'Go with you where?'

'When I leave: you can come overseas with me, to Europe.'

The proposition didn't seem to warrant much consideration. 'They'd never let me out of the country.'

'If you were to marry me. . .'

She looked at him for a while. 'Is that a proposal of marriage?' she asked, and the idea seemed to amuse her in spite of her seriousness.

'It would just be a formality. I want, very much, to

help you.'

'And what am I to do overseas?'

'Begin a new life.'

'A life like yours and people like you? Never at ease, discontented, always recalling the past and yearning, always chewing the cud of your memories? And always with the same self-reproach gnawing at you?' The head turned away on the pillow; the hand limp on the bedspread; the gold bracelet now too big for the wrist. . . The hiss of tyres on wet tarmac, a policeman waving them on.

'Is this life of yours so much better?'

'It's more or less the same. They also brood over their memories and their grievances; they keep returning to their hurts, and dream of the past and believe it'll all come back again. But it won't; nothing comes back.' She jumped up, impatient. 'You're trapped in the web of the past, all of you, here and over there. Hendrik and Johannes —I have to say this to you, there has to be someone I can tell— my own brothers dashed off with a mouthful of threadbare slogans, they set off to regain a world they themselves hadn't even known. They've been taken away and we'll never see them again — God knows what will happen to them, I can't bring myself to think about it. But it's senseless, worthless, useless; it's devoid of any meaning. If I could only believe in it like my parents do, it would at least be tolerable, but it's words: that's all — words. There's nothing at all.'

After a pause he said: 'Will it all be as it was, now that they've been taken away?'

'One doesn't lose hope so easily. So many people have already been caught and killed or taken away, and then someone else starts afresh.' She laughed abruptly. 'We should really be thankful that they did nothing more than take the three of them away, just those three, and that the rest of us were spared.'

'Were there other people involved?'

'Who isn't involved in it? Haven't you understood anything yet? One night when there was no moon they buried some chests here on the farm, in the old cemetery: they prised up the gravestones with crowbars. They. . .' She broke off impatiently. 'Agh, why am I telling you all this? You've spent three days with us without noticing what was going on around you: you've wandered through the whole house and all over the farmyard without seeing or hearing anything. It's better that you just go away in ignorance. In any case, you don't need to know anything.'

'And you want to be left behind with this?' She shook her head with unexpected decisiveness.

'When something becomes irrevocable, you have to recognize the fact and accept it. It doesn't help to kick and struggle, all your tears and your prayers won't help. You must go on with your life, as well or as badly as you can. It's life that's unyielding, implacable, it's not me. The old world has disappeared and it will never, in all eternity, come back, even if we give our lives to try to regain it. We must learn to live in the new world.'

He must go, he thought: time was running out. But he didn't move.

'You must go,' she said, echoing his thoughts.

'Yes.'

'Are you glad?'

'I don't know.'

'Will you still remember us when you're back home?'

'Oh yes, I'll remember you. I'll remember you just as

you are now, standing here chopping wood with splinters in your hair.' He smiled. 'And I'll always be concerned about you.'

She too smiled and shook her head. 'You don't have to be: I can look after myself.'

'But what will become of you?'

'I'm also going away,' she said but she spoke so swiftly and casually that he only just caught the words.

'Where to?'

'I don't know yet. I only know that I'm not going to stay here on the farm.' She looked at him, hesitating. 'I haven't told anyone about this yet, not even Paul. My parents know nothing at all about it; it'll grieve them enough when it happens: there's no point in upsetting them beforehand. Promise you'll not say a word to anyone?'

Of course I won't. But what will you do? How will you live?'

'I don't know,' she said again. 'But I don't mean to be trapped in memories like everyone else here is; I don't want to spend my life looking over my shoulder. I want to make my contribution, not sit on one side and perish in a world of dreams. I want to achieve something; I want to live. . .'

'Do you realize what you're undertaking?'

'Yes, I realize. But I'm young, I'm strong, I can put my hand to anything. Just as long as you've got courage and believe in what you're doing, it doesn't matter what happens to you. I'm not afraid. There's nothing I'm afraid of.'

He knew that she was speaking the truth. 'I think you're unwise,' he said, 'but I don't expect I'll be able to convince you of that.'

'No, you won't.'

'I still wish that there was something, anything, I could do to help you.'

'You've listened to me, that's more than enough. I only wish that I could make you understand, but you haven't the vaguest idea what I'm talking about: I can see it simply by looking at your face. But try, if you really want to do something for me, just try, so that there'll be at least one person who understands.'

'I'll try,' he said after a long silence.

'We're speaking different languages,' she said slowly, 'even though the words sound the same. We remain strangers to one another, and you'll never understand what I'm talking about. But try.'

She had turned her back on him and was leaning against the piled-up logs, her head on her arm.

'George!' called Hattingh from the house.

'You'll miss your train,' she said. She wiped her forehead with her hand, tried to pluck the wood-chips from her hair, and brushed off those which had stuck to her clothes, but her movements were slow and absent-minded.

'George!' Hattingh called again.

George went swiftly up to her. 'Come with me,' he said. 'There's still time, you can still get away. You'll be under no obligation to me whatsoever, I only want to help you. Why must you battle on here when you could be happy?'

'No,' she said, almost to herself. 'You understand nothing at all.' She rubbed her forehead with her hand and looked around. She rested her hands briefly on the split logs and the axe, and walked away from him without looking back.

Hattingh carried his suitcase to the car and pressed his hand. Mrs Hattingh threw her arms around his neck and pulled him to her to kiss him. Only Paul stood apart and looked without interest at the preparations for his departure, as if they concerned some stranger.

'Now where on earth has Carla got to?' asked Mrs Hattingh.

'I don't know, Ma.'

'Carla and I have already said goodbye, Mrs Hattingh.'

'But she could at least be here now that you're actually leaving. I don't know where she's gone.' Out of politeness they were trying to hide their own grief, as they stood outside to see him on his way.

He switched on the engine and looked at them for the last time where they stood on the kitchen steps against the bare wall: Hattingh, his wife, and Paul. Then Carla appeared in the doorway behind them and silently raised her hand in a farewell. She had come. He raised his hand in answer and the Hattinghs waved at him without realizing that she was standing behind them.

He turned the car in the yard and drove out of the gate to the main road. He saw the veld, occasional trees, the clouds hiding the sun and birds swerving low in front of him. He had to drive slowly along the neglected road, but there was enough time: he would catch his train. The plane left that evening; tomorrow morning he'd be home.